PORTRAIT OF A POISON PEN ARTIST:

This was one of her bad days, when loneliness overcame her and loathing of the whole world.

At breakfast she looked at her husband with icy contempt. She could scarcely stand the sight of him. "Get your lunch downtown today," she told him curtly. "I won't be here."

She drove to town, went on an extravagant shopping spree, lunched at an expensive restaurant, and stopped for cocktails at an expensive bar, but they didn't raise her spirits. Her mood was even more sullen and bitter than before. Driving back, she brooded about Lucia. She'd written violent things about her in letters to the bank president, but nothing had happened. She pounded the steering wheel in frustration. The goddamned fools, keeping a tramp like that at the bank!

She had come to believe her own lies about Lucia.

Later, at the typewriter, her fingers flew over the keys in a letter to Lucia filled with savage, obscene threats. Just wait till she gets this letter, Inez gloated. It will scare the bitch to death!

She felt better now, secure in a sense of power she could exercise at will.

DORIS MILES DISNEY
BLACK MAIL

Kensington Publishing Corp.
475 Park Avenue South
New York, NY 10016

ZEBRA BOOKS
KENSINGTON PUBLISHING CORP.

ZEBRA BOOKS

are published by

Kensington Publishing Corp.
475 Park Avenue South
New York, NY 10016

First Zebra Books printing: May, 1989

Printed in the United States of America

*This book is dedicated
to the Postal Inspection Service.
The more I find out about it
the more respect and admiration I have
for its achievements.*

Chapter One

It had been a dismal November day, raining off and on and pouring a little before ten that night, when Lucia Ruyter, the collar of her raincoat turned up, the hat that matched it pulled down over her face, ran the whole length of the block from the Corner Shop to where she had parked her car around the next corner. She kept her head down to avoid the gusts of rain the wind flung in her face, but, even so, when she rounded the next corner and started across the street she didn't rush blindly off the curb, she stopped first to look in both directions and make sure no cars were coming toward her.

Afterward, this precaution made what followed seem all the more inexplicable to her. One moment the street was deserted, no cars, no people in sight, just the pavement glistening black in the rain between her and her car on the far side of it. Then, as she started across, a car swooped down on her seemingly from out of nowhere, traveling much too fast for the weather conditions, heading straight for her, the headlights pinning her in the middle of the road like a paralyzed bird or rabbit, her startled face, turned toward them, surely visible above her dark raincoat. But the driver showed no awareness of her, no horn sounded, there were just the glaring headlights to warn her of the car's approach.

She screamed at the top of her lungs. Then, in the last split second before the wheels would have gone over her, her paralysis vanished and she jumped back so that it was only the bumper or perhaps the fender that caught her, spun her around violently, and threw her to the pavement.

The car didn't stop. She couldn't remember afterward having heard a squeal of tires to indicate that the brakes had ever been applied.

But she couldn't be sure of that in the shock of what had happened. She couldn't be sure of anything for the next few minutes. A door slammed somewhere, and a man ran out to help her as she struggled to rise. Then more people appeared, cars stopped, it was astonishing how quickly a crowd managed to gather on a street deserted only moments ago.

A blue uniform loomed in front of the girl while she was protesting that she was all right, only bruised and shaken up.

"Hospital," she heard. "You can't tell, miss what injuries you've had. Hospital's the place for you."

A police cruiser materialized out of the rainy darkness, and somehow, dazed and helpless, she found herself in it and on the way to the hospital, trying to give the patrolman at the wheel a coherent account of what had happened.

An examination, sedatives, something soothing for her cuts and bruises. Against her will she was tucked into a hospital bed for the night, and the next morning, when she complained of a headache to the resident doctor, she ended up in the X-ray room.

But by afternoon the hospital conceded that she would be allowed to go home with Mrs. Aitken, her motherly

8

landlady, who arrived with fresh clothes to replace the torn and mud-stained things she had been wearing last night.

"You didn't let my mother know?" Lucia asked, when she had eased her lame, sore body into Mrs. Aitken's car and they had started home.

"No, I didn't. The hospital seemed to feel that you'd be all right, so I thought I'd leave that up to you. If I called, it would upset her far more than for you to do it."

"What good sense you showed." Lucia squeezed the older woman's arm affectionately. "She certainly would have been upset and all for nothing. I'm fine now except for my bruises."

"Just the same, you're going to bed the minute we get in the house," Mrs. Aitken informed her.

"Honestly, I'm—" Lucia caught Mrs. Aitken's eye and subsided on that subject, changing it by asking about her car. A police officer had brought it home and it was now in the garage, Mrs. Aitken said.

When they reached the older woman's big, old-fashioned house, where Lucia had an apartment in the one-story ell, the girl did not, after all, go to bed immediately. A police cruiser stood out in front with an officer at the wheel waiting for them. He introduced himself as Sergeant Drake and said he had just arrived, having phoned the hospital and learned that Miss Ruyter was on her way home.

He accompanied them into Lucia's apartment, standing in silence near the door while Mrs. Aitken settled her on the sofa with a pillow under her head and went into the kitchen to make her a cup of tea. Then the sergeant sat down near Lucia, took out a notebook, and said, "Now, Miss Ruyter, let's see if we can't get the whole story straight on what happened last night."

"You haven't found out anything yet about the car

9

that hit me?"

He shook his head. "We've got nothing to go on so far. It seems no one in the neighborhood saw it, there were no witnesses at all. The man who got to you first said he'd opened his front door to call his dog and heard you scream. But all he saw as he ran out to you was the taillight disappearing down the street." After a pause the sergeant asked, "What can you tell me about the car yourself, Miss Ruyter?"

She said slowly, "Light-colored, I think. That's all. The headlights"—she shivered—"were overwhelming, turned on full beam, bearing down on me. It was—horrible."

"I guess it was," he said sympathetically.

"And going very fast. The most reckless driving you ever saw, Sergeant, considering how hard it was raining last night." Indignation sounded in Lucia's voice. "If I'd been killed by that car, it would have been just plain murder."

The sergeant, a stolid man, said with more feeling than he had so far shown, "You've got the right idea, there, Miss Ruyter. I'm always ready to throw the book at these hit-and-run drivers when I catch them!"

He went stolid again, pencil poised over his notebook. "You said a light car. You thinking of tan or gray or what?"

"I don't know. It happened so quickly—"

"Big car?"

"Oh dear." She sat up, feeling at a disadvantage lying on the sofa while the sergeant questioned her. "I don't know—except that it certainly wasn't a small car like a Volkswagen or something. It looked enormous to me, but—" She broke off. This was hopeless, she was no use at all. She couldn't even say if the driver was a man or a woman.

10

"Well, let's go back a little, maybe that will help you to remember something more," the sergeant said encouragingly. "You were crossing the street to your car. Where were you before that?"

"At the Corner Shop with some girls I work with at the bank. Yesterday was Thursday, and the bank's open until nine Thursday nights, you know. We'd stopped in for coffee. They were in another car, so I left them outside the Corner Shop and started for my car. . . ."

Carefully, trying to remember every detail, Lucia described what followed. But none of it, she knew, would help in locating the car that had hit her, although the sergeant made some notes on what she told him.

At the end he said, "We examined the area last night, Miss Ruyter, and again by daylight this morning. Not a thing. No skid marks from the tires to show the driver tried to put on the brakes, no broken glass from a headlight, nothing at all."

"I told the officer last night that I thought it was just the bumper that hit me."

"Well then, the car's not marked or damaged in any way, you see." His gesture conveyed the hopelessness of trying to locate it.

For a moment Lucia came close to saying. "Too bad I didn't let it really bang me up so there'd be something to go on," but checked herself in using sarcasm as an outlet for her sense of frustration. It wasn't this stolid sergeant's fault that the hit-and-run driver had left behind no evidence for the police.

She'd been lucky not to have been seriously injured or killed, she reminded herself. Be thankful for that, without worrying too much about whether or not they caught the driver.

The sergeant said next, "Considering what the weather was last night, Miss Ruyter, it's possible the driver didn't

11

even see you, let alone realize he'd hit you."

"In that case, won't he come forward today when he sees it in the paper?"

"Well, you'd think so. But then again, some people'd do anything to keep out of trouble. He knows you weren't hurt seriously, he may just forget it."

"I can't imagine doing that if I hit anyone," Lucia commented. A moment later she went on, "Furthermore, I don't see how it could have happened like that. I was pinned down squarely by the headlights. Unless the driver was blind he couldn't miss seeing me, and he'd also have to be deaf not to hear me, the way I screamed. It was almost as if—" She stopped short, astonished at what she had been about to say.

"Almost as if what, Miss Ruyter?"

"As if—well, the driver were in a trance," she substituted for what she had been about to say.

She had to keep that to herself. The sergeant would think she was hysterical or something if she told him that, looking back on last night, the thought had suddenly struck her that it was almost as if the driver had meant to run her down.

What a thing that would be to say! Even to think . . .

Mrs. Aitken came in just then with the tea.

The sergeant said no, thank you, when asked if he would have some. Within a few minutes he left, telling Lucia he hoped she'd be all right in a day or two and that he'd let her know if he found out anything about her accident.

By Monday the girl was back at the Fairmount Trust Company where she had been promoted recently to assistant treasurer of the Loan and Discount Department and reveled in her new job.

The following week she went home for Thanksgiving but didn't mention what had happened to her mother. In

12

another week or two, busy as she was with many friends and activities to crowd her life, it began to fade from her memory. Christmas dimmed it still more. By the time the new year began she rarely thought of it, and then almost as if it were something that had happened to someone else.

Chapter Two

It remained fresh in Inez Blaine's mind, emblazoned on her memory. She would forget none of it, coming out of the drugstore across from the Corner Shop, seeing Lucia start to run through the rain, getting in her car and following the girl without turning on her headlights, stopping near the corner to watch her start across the street—she hadn't known until Lucia stepped off the curb why she had followed her, what she thought it might lead to.

Then blind hatred took over, turning her car into a weapon in her hands. . . .

When she arrived home she brushed aside Alec's efforts at conversation and, shaking from head to toe, hurried upstairs to Gibb's room, where she stood looking out a window at the stormy night. She couldn't have said even then if she was glad or sorry that Lucia, jumping back, had managed to escape with what must be relatively minor injuries. She only knew that she hated her twice as much as before, that what had happened was all Lucia's fault. Through what she had done to Gibb, she had driven his mother to attempted murder.

The next morning at the breakfast table, Alec read aloud in a shocked voice the item in the paper on Lucia's accident, and went on to deplore the cold-blooded behavior of the driver and of hit-and-run drivers in general.

Inez said nothing, but he paid no attention to this. He was used to having her speak only when she felt like it.

The evening paper carried a smaller item that said Lucia had been released from the hospital, and that so far the police hadn't located the car that hit her.

Inez felt safe after reading it. No one would ever find out that she had tried to commit murder.

But a sense of safety wasn't enough, she discovered, not for very long. As the days passed her hatred of Lucia again took possession of her, preying on her nerves, destroying her rest and her peace of mind. Now it had a double edge, with Gibb one edge, her brush with murder the other.

Gibb didn't come home for Christmas. Before he left he'd said he wouldn't, that, aside from the money it would cost, he'd be too new in his job to take the time off to come all the way back across the country.

But it was their first Christmas without him. And how was he spending it, so far away, alone among strangers?

Inez would have been happy to have plunged the knife with which Alec carved their Christmas turkey into Lucia's heart if she had been given the chance.

Gibb phoned Christmas night and told his mother about the new friends in Seattle who'd had him for dinner and what a nice day he'd had. He sounded cheerful as he went on to tell her how much he was enjoying the hi-fi set they'd sent him for Christmas, but Inez felt certain he was just trying to put a good face on things to make her feel better.

Alec had written him about Lucia's accident, but Gibb didn't ask how she was, didn't mention her name.

That showed what his real feelings were. Lucia had

16

hurt him so much that he couldn't bear to make the least reference to her.

Somehow, somehow, she would pay the girl back. How? She didn't know but she would think of a way. . . .

On a day in January, working as a volunteer at the Visiting Nurse Association's office, she thought of one.

Inez, active in community affairs, taking intense pride in the prominence they brought her, had been a board member of the agency for the past three years and devoted a considerable amount of her time to its affairs, enjoying the sense of importance it gave her and the plaudits of the other board members for the volunteer work she did there.

The senior nurse and her assistant were out on calls that January afternoon a week after New Year's when Inez, alone in the office, making up a case record, found in the nurse's notes a statement that was like an arrow pointing the way to her.

"Mr. Gardiner," the nurse had written, "says he has been unable to find work since he lost his job at Armstrong's Garage as a result of a number of anonymous phone calls to his boss about him."

Inez stopped typing when she read this, sat back from the desk, and lit a cigarette, her eyes narrowed in thought.

Anonymous phone calls—Lucia's job, Lucia's promotion that had pleased her so much, according to Alec. Well. The bank was fussy about its employees' moral character. Couldn't that of a young woman, one who was attractive, unmarried, be easily torn down? But how could it be worked? Disguise her voice on the phone? Wasn't that easier said than done? If Mr. Hasbrouck should recognize it, why, Alec's job would be out the window and where would he get another like it at his age?

She shook her head. She wouldn't dare risk a series of

17

calls to Mr. Hasbrouck.

Her fingers beat a nervous tattoo on the desk. There must be some way to get around using the phone.

There was. Her eyes sparkled with triumph as it occurred to her, and her hand shot out to the drawer where paper was kept. But with the drawer open she hesitated, looking down into it. It held a plentiful supply of white paper used for second sheets without the agency letterhead, but the envelopes were useless. They had Visiting Nurse Association and the address printed on them.

"Anyway . . . stop and think," she admonished herself. "Don't rush into this. Think of all the angles, make sure there's nothing that could give you away. You've waited weeks, months actually, you can wait a few days more. You'll be here Monday, you're here every Monday and Thursday and sometimes other days when volunteers don't come in. You often have the office to yourself for hours at a time. Think of everything, what to say, how to say it, nothing that could be disproved, watch what dates and places you use, pump Alec for all he's worth. One letter probably wouldn't be enough to get Lucia fired, not with Mr. Hasbrouck thinking she's so wonderful."

Inez' gaze settled on the Underwood standard in front of her. She would type the letters, of course. Handwriting could be checked on. What about typewriters? Hadn't she read or seen something in a movie that indicated there were ways to tell what kind of a typewriter a letter was written on?

She eyed the Underwood doubtfully. If a fuss should be made over the letters, there'd be no reason for anyone to check on the VNA typewriter, but still . . .

Presently her face cleared. She had found an answer to the problem of the typewriter.

Tonight she would start pumping Alec about Lucia. He'd always liked the girl and was such a spineless little worm that he hadn't stopped liking her because of the way she'd treated Gibb. Just the other day he'd mentioned her, something about her skiing at North Conway over the week end. Well, Inez had shut him up fast at the time, but tonight she wouldn't. Then, over the week end, she'd plan what to say in her first letter. It would depend, of course, on what information she got out of Alec and what, if she put her mind to it, she could find out from other sources. Mrs. Aitken, for instance. She was perfectly fatuous about Lucia. Ever since the girl had rented the apartment from her, she'd been telling everyone how nice she was, how good in her job, and what a perfect joy to have for a tenant. Why, since Lucia had been with her, Mrs. Aitken had been doing all sorts of expensive things to the apartment, having the chimney repaired and the closed-up fireplace in the living room reopened, the whole place papered and painted, open bookshelves built in on either side of the fireplace. It was all perfectly ridiculous. She'd helped Lucia make new draperies for the living room and, although she'd always rented the apartment completely furnished, she'd meekly relegated things of her own to the attic to make way for some of Lucia's and even let the girl take down old family pictures to hang modern prints on the walls.

The way Mrs. Aitken went on about her, it was all too apparent that Lucia had pulled the wool over her eyes good and proper. Mrs. Aitken was blind as a bat when it came to the girl's true nature.

If more than one letter had to be written, there was a board meeting next week. She would get Mrs. Aitken talking about Lucia then.

Too excited to sit at the desk, Inez stood up and walked around the room with light quick steps, carried out of herself in an ecstasy of planning. She came to a halt at the front window. How she'd fix Lucia, she told herself delightedly. How she'd fix her!

There was only one small flaw in her plan. Lucia would never know who had brought about her downfall. She'd be out of the bank, thrown out on her ear, and would have to go home to Massachusetts dragging her tail behind her, but she'd never know who brought it about.

Well, that couldn't be helped. Inez hummed to herself, contemplating her own cleverness with rapture.

But then her humming died away and her mouth turned sour with discontent. She went back to the desk and sat down, feeling heavy, suddenly, with middle age and loneliness. When this was all over, Lucia out of the bank and gone from Fairmount, Gibb would still be on the other side of the continent, driven away from his mother by Lucia's treatment of him.

Inez closed her eyes in anguish, remembering that day in October when Gibb had told her about his new job. He'd picked a time when Alec wasn't home—they'd always been so close, Gibb and she—wanting to tell her about it before he mentioned it to his father. It had been such a shock that she just couldn't help breaking down, crying terribly and begging him not to go away.

He wouldn't tell her at first his real reason for changing jobs. He'd kept insisting that the new one had more future in it, paid better, gave him a chance to see a different part of the country. He'd talked about how often he'd write, how she must come out and visit him— as if that could begin to compare with having him live at home!—and in the end it was she who'd brought up Lucia's name. It was only two months since Lucia had turned him down, and although he'd pretended at the time that it hadn't been too great a blow she'd known better, as only a mother who adored her son could know;

she'd known how sensitive Gibb was, how deep his feelings ran. And finally, when she'd brought Lucia into it, he'd admitted that he did want to get away for a while on account of her, that Fairmount wasn't big enough for both of them.

Inez had argued and pleaded, pointing out that a girl as selfish as Lucia wouldn't have made him happy anyway, that he'd had a narrow escape from what would have been a poor marriage, that if he'd only look at it that way, try to think about it calmly instead of letting his feelings run away with him, he'd be thankful that Lucia had turned him down and stay right here in Fairmount where he had his comfortable home and a mother who would do everything she could to make it up to him and help him to forget.

But Gibb, poor boy, wouldn't listen to her, was too hurt to listen. He'd insisted he must get away for a while.

And now he was in Seattle, and her heart broke every time she went into his empty room at home.

This was Lucia's doing, uppity young bitch that she was, holding her head so high and thinking, no doubt, that she was too good for Gibb, when the truth was that the girl hadn't yet been born who was good enough for her fine, brilliant son.

But Lucia would get paid back.

"God, how I hate, her," Inez said aloud. "Hate her, hate her!"

The front door opened and footsteps sounded in the hall. She turned back to the typewriter and appeared to be deep in a study of Mrs. Burdette's notes when the senior nurse came in and said, "Well, Mrs. Blaine, how's it going?"

"Fine," Inez replied, and Mrs. Burdette, after a moment's conversation, went on across the room to her own office.

21

A smile of satisfaction spread across Inez' face as she began to type. She'd just thought of something else she could do to Lucia that would jar her out of feeling so superior and pleased with herself.

A little later she smiled again as still another satisfying thought struck her. Perhaps when this was over and Lucia gone from Fairmount, Gibb would listen to reason and come home.

Chapter Three

When Lucia got home from work the following Tuesday afternoon she found three pieces of mail in her box, and glanced through them in the vestibule while she was unlocking her door. The first was a letter in her mother's sprawling hand, the second a bill from a department store, the third, with her name and address typed on the face of the envelope, gave no information about itself. An ad of some sort, she thought, opening the door.

She read first her mother's letter full of the small cheerful news of home, opened the department store bill to sigh over the total, and then opened her third piece of mail.

It began with the salutation, "Dear Miss Ruyter," but that was the only normal thing about it. The rest she read with shocked disbelief that anyone could have written such horrible, obscene things to her.

Her face flamed with shame and anger as she read it a second time. Who could have written it? Someone she knew—the knowledge it displayed of her activities made that plain—but who could it be?

Some man, she thought. No woman could possibly have written the things that were in the letter about her behavior with men. None of them were true, but at the moment that was beside the point.

When she was calmer she looked at the envelope. The typing told her nothing, the postmark told her the letter had been mailed in Fairmount yesterday, the time of cancellation 7 P.M.

Lucia resisted an impulse to tear the letter up. Instead she locked it away in a suitcase in her closet. She couldn't have said why she kept it, what she meant to do about it. Nothing, really, she thought. But still she kept it.

The next morning not long after the bank opened Mr. Hasbrouck, the president, summoned Lucia to his office. She wondered, as she obeyed the summons, what he wanted to see her about. Was it to give her another fatherly talk on how young she was for the responsible position he had entrusted to her? Something like that, she thought.

But when she entered his office, closed the door after her as he asked her to do, and sat down opposite his desk suddenly she felt uneasy. The grave expression on his plump face told her that more than a pep talk lay behind his summons. A mistake in her work? A loan application she shouldn't have approved?

Mr. Hasbrouck waited until she was seated and then said, "I received a letter about you yesterday, Lucia. A very unpleasant anonymous letter."

In spite of having received one herself, Lucia was least of all prepared for this. Color flooded her face, she opened her mouth to speak, but no words came.

Mr. Hasbrouck, pompous but basically kind, shared her embarrassment. He fiddled with papers on his desk, straightened his pen holder, and went on, "Anonymous letters belong in the wastebasket, of course, but still—I thought you'd want to know about it. I needn't tell you, I guess, that I don't believe a word it said."

Lucia found her voice. "I got one too yesterday, Mr. Hasbrouck. About my behavior with men." She

24

paused. "Did yours mention my going skiing the week end after New Year's at North Conway?"

"Well, yes. Among other things."

"What other things, Mr. Hasbrouck?"

When he hesitated Lucia said, "I would like to know what else it said. It's my reputation that's being defamed."

"Yes, that's right. But the whole thing—as I told you, anonymous letters belong in the wastebasket. However . . . a man named Jack Morse came into it."

"I go out with him now and then." Lucia's color rose still more as she recalled what her letter had said about her relations with Jack Morse. She gathered courage to ask, "Was your letter obscene, Mr. Hasbrouck?"

He looked startled, shook his head. "Oh no. There was profanity but that was all."

"Mine was very obscene."

"Oh." Mr. Hasbrouck fiddled some more with the papers on his desk, looked at Lucia with a deeply troubled expression, and said, "Somebody certainly has it in for you. I suppose you have a pretty good idea who it is."

"I haven't the least idea," she told him.

He eyed her incredulously. "But, Lucia, it must be somebody you've had trouble with. Who else would do a thing like that to you?"

"I don't know. All I know is that I've had no trouble with anyone."

The bank president rallied and tried to be helpful. "Well, let's see if we can't figure it out between us. I wondered when I read my letter if it hadn't been written by a woman. Out of jealousy, perhaps. A young man who liked you better than her."

"There's no one like that. It couldn't be a woman, anyway. No woman would write the things that were in my letter."

"Then what about—"

25

"No, not a man that I've had dates with, Mr. Hasbrouck. I'd know if it were anyone like that."

He turned his attention reluctantly to her new job, asking if anyone had showed resentment toward her over it.

"No, there's been none that I know of," Lucia said.

Mr. Hasbrouck's "Well . . ." had an inconclusive sound. There was no other sound it could have, Lucia reflected unhappily. She could and did explain in detail the innocent nature of her skiing trip, and added that whatever else his letter said about her having improper relations with men was untrue. She said all this, and her voice steadied as she said it with the effort she made to instill some dignity into the wretched occasion. But in the end, no matter what she said, it was all inconclusive.

Mr. Hasbrouck assured her again that he didn't believe a word that was in his letter, and then told her not to worry about it or mention it to anyone. The less said about the whole affair the better. He was going to destroy his letter, he advised her to do the same.

When Lucia said that of course she wouldn't mention it to anyone, Mr. Hasbrouck looked relieved. Naturally, she thought. Gossip centering on one of the bank's employees would be abhorrent to Mr. Hasbrouck. And over him hung the shadow of Mr. Jenner, chairman of the board of directors.

At the end of the interview the girl went back to her desk in a daze. She had an enemy, someone who hated her enough to try to destroy her reputation and perhaps cause her to lose her job, and she didn't know who it was.

She thought about it the rest of the day, the rest of the week. Whatever she was doing it was never far from her mind, coloring her thoughts and feeling toward everyone she knew, lending a new dimension of doubt to her relationship with them.

Friday evening she went to a dance with Jack Morse,

whom she'd liked before the letters arrived, but she spent so much time wondering what he was like inside that the evening was spoiled for her and she didn't care if she ever saw him again.

Wednesday morning brought another summons to the bank president's office. Lucia steeled herself as she obeyed it, and it was well that she did. Mr. Hasbrouck had found a second letter waiting for him last night.

"Is it like the last one?" she asked.

"Yes, it is."

Their interview was a repeat performance of the previous one, Mr. Hasbrouck fiddling with papers again, thoroughly uncomfortable about the whole thing. But no, Lucia thought, it wasn't quite the same. It seemed to her that she caught a shade of reserve in his manner toward her that hadn't been there last week.

Presently he remarked, "The writer is definitely keeping an eye on you. Did you go to a dance Friday night?"

"Yes, at the club with Jack Morse. Anyone could have seen me there. Is that what the letter's about?"

The bank president nodded. "It says you went to the dance with him and to his apartment in Dunston afterward, and that you didn't get home until nearly daylight."

"Oh no, Mr. Hasbrouck!" Lucia exclaimed. "That part's a lie! After the dance we did go to Dunston but just to Sinclair's, that all-night restaurant on Lewis Street. We got there at two o'clock, were there about an hour, and then Jack drove me home. I was home by three-thirty. That was fairly late, perhaps, but after all it was a Friday night when I could sleep the next morning."

Mr. Hasbrouck smiled faintly. "I'm getting old, Lucia. Couldn't keep such hours myself no matter what night it was." After a pause he said, "You've had a whole week to think about this. Don't you have any idea who's doing it?"

"None. Even though I think about it all the time." Lucia went on, "But I've got to do something about it. You've had two letters, I've had one, and it seems they're going to keep coming. I'll have to go to the police."

Mr. Hasbrouck looked perturbed. "The police? Well, I don't really know what they could do when you can't name anyone for them to investigate. It might end up in a lot of talk that would be very unpleasant for you."

And for the bank, Lucia thought. She asked, "What do you think I should do about it, Mr. Hasbrouck? I can't let it go on. It's a serious thing to have my reputation maligned like this."

"Of course it is. But I don't know what to advise, Lucia. If you go to the police and anything leaks out about it, well . . ." His gaze shifted to the ceiling. "You know how people talk, how quick they are to say that where there's smoke there's fire. I'm a lot older than you, old enough to be your father, and I know how bad it might be. There's no way, you see, for you to disprove some of the statements in the letters."

"I can disprove the one about my going to Jack's apartment the other night," Lucia replied firmly. "The waitress and cashier at the restaurant saw us there."

The bank president made a steeple of his fingers and regarded it in silence for a moment before he said, "But—uh—after you left the restaurant can you prove what time you got home? Understand," he went on quickly, "I don't question it in the least myself. I'm only trying to point out to you how difficult your position would be if you set out to disprove what the letter says. Your most harmless action could be twisted around and—well—it's hard to say what is the best course for you to take. If you could only go to the police—if they're the ones to see—and give them a name or two to work on, it would be a different story. But the way it is . . ."

28

As he went on talking Lucia felt as if she were trying to fight her way out of a net; and that the more she fought the more entangled in it she became.

It wasn't, she told herself, that Mr. Hasbrouck didn't believe her or that he was trying to set himself up as the mentor of her private affairs. He was genuinely concerned for her, although some, at least, of his concern must be on behalf of the bank, stemming from the fact that she, his protégé, had incurred the hatred of someone unsavory enough to write anonymous letters and therefore capable of heaven knew what other irregular behavior.

Then, as he pressed her again on the identity of the writer, she felt that, no matter what she said about not knowing who it was, he found it difficult to believe her.

Did he perhaps think she was covering up for someone?

It came to her shatteringly that if he thought that, then he must also think that she'd done something to give someone a hold on her.

She was almost in tears by the time the interview ended. And had reached no decision toward taking action on the letters, having agreed to wait a little longer. If there were more, they might give her a clue to who was writing them, Mr. Hasbrouck suggested, something concrete to go on. In the meantime, he would keep his second letter. "Although I'd really prefer to put it where it belongs, in the wastebasket with the other one," he said.

But regardless of what he said Lucia felt that a cloud hung over her, a question mark came into Mr. Hasbrouck's mind when he thought of her.

She didn't have to wait until the next week to see if the letters were going to be kept up. Friday afternoon she found one in her own mail that repeated what the first one had said about her morals, and then went on to the dance she had attended with Jack Morse, sparing no obscenity in describing her behavior in his apartment after the dance.

Lucia, handling it as fastidiously as if it might contaminate her, locked it away with its companion. Then she moved to a window and stood looking out at the children playing in the yard next door. They were carefree, she thought. They didn't know that such letters as she had received could exist.

Indignation shook her as she stood at the window. She wasn't going to put up with this much longer, no matter what Mr. Hasbrouck said about the gossip she'd stir up. It was turning into a persecution.

The following Wednesday morning the summons she expected came from the bank president. But this time he wasn't alone when she entered the office. Seated beside his desk was Mr. Jenner, chairman of the board, who had already, Lucia inferred from Mr. Hasbrouck's dejected expression, cut the bank president down to what he regarded as the proper size.

Trying to calm herself, she drew in a deep breath and said, "Good morning." Mr. Hasbrouck's smile, weak though it was, offered encouragement, and his glance approved of her tailored suit, minimum amount of make-up, and hair style that gave her dignity. Her whole appearance should, he thought, impress Claude favorably.

"Good morning, Lucia," he replied. "Won't you— uh—sit down?"

The little old board chairman with his bitter eyes and nutcracker jaw merely nodded at Lucia. She sat down.

"I've had another letter," Mr. Hasbrouck began. "Mr. Jenner received one too. They're both alike."

"Mr. Jenner too . . . ?" Lucia's voice faded out.

"Yes indeed," the board chairman snapped. "And I must say I'm surprised I haven't been told about what was going on before this. But now that I have been brought into it, we're going to get to the bottom of it without any more shilly-shallying. There's been too much of it already. After all, you hold a responsible job here at the bank, Miss Ruyter. It's not three months ago that you were promoted to it on Mr. Hasbrouck's recommendation. I had misgivings myself," he eyed her stonily, "I thought you were too young for the job. But Mr. Hasbrouck said no, he assured me you were very steady and capable. And now we have this. Mr. Hasbrouck and I have been talking it over, and we want to be fair about it. We don't think it's got a thing to do with your new job, no one else was even in the running for it. What do you think about that yourself?"

"It can't be my job." Lucia kept her voice low so that the tremor in it would be less noticeable. "I told Mr. Hasbrouck so. I—" She stopped, her nervousness so acute that she lost the thread of what she had been about to say.

As her silence prolonged itself, Mr. Jenner demanded testily, "Well, now that we're all in agreement that it isn't someone at the bank, who is writing the letters, Miss Ruyter?"

Lucia, very pale, replied, "I don't know, Mr. Jenner."

He leaned forward, looking not unlike a bird of prey about to pounce. "Are you going to sit there and tell me the same story you told Mr. Hasbrouck about not knowing who's got it in for you enough to write these letters?" He shook his head, his mouth a tight line beneath his pointed nose. "I can't accept that, Miss Ruyter. Nobody with any sense could. Who are you covering up for? What have you got yourself mixed up in?"

Although this was an attitude she had thought herself prepared for, still it shocked Lucia when it was put into words. Then anger came to her rescue, overriding her other emotions. She said in a cold, clear voice, "Mr.

31

Jenner, I've always been regarded as a reputable person. I am not lying when I say I have no idea who's writing the letters. It's the plain truth."

He looked somewhat taken aback for a moment. Then, testy again, he said, "But you must have had trouble with someone who feels you've done them an injury. How could this happen and you know nothing about it?"

"I don't know," Lucia said.

She wasn't asked for her resignation that day. Actually, she wasn't asked for it Thursday when Mr. Hasbrouck received another letter, this one sent to him at the bank.

Mr. Jenner, making daily appearances this week, arrived in his office while he was reading it. Lucia was sent for.

With Mr. Jenner at his elbow the bank president felt unequal to the discussion of the matter. He handed the letter to Lucia.

It was brief. It said: "How much longer are you going to keep that tramp Lucia Ruyter at the bank? Haven't you heard the talk about her and Roger Acres who used to work for Industrial Chemicals? He knew she had no more morals than an alley cat and got himself transferred to Rochester to get rid of her. But I guess you don't care about that. You think you're a little tin god when it comes to picking out your employees. Why don't you get wise to yourself?"

Lucia looked at the two men. "This is a lie, every word of it. Roger Acres and I were just casually acquainted and—" She had to break off in mid-sentence. She would have cried with humiliation if she had tried to go on.

"Of course we realize it's a lie," Mr. Hasbrouck made haste to say, using the plural pronoun out of kindness.

The girl's glance went from him to Mr. Jenner, whose mouth was clamped shut. He wasn't going to offer a word of reassurance.

Pride stiffened her. Addressing herself to the bank president, she said, "I can't put up with this a minute longer, Mr. Hasbrouck. I'm going straight to the police about it. Since I don't know what that will lead to, I'll hand in my resignation first. Dated as of today."

Mr. Jenner looked relieved, then discontented. "No, that won't do," he declared. "It'll bring on a lot of talk right here at the bank, the very thing we're trying to avoid. If you want to go ahead with it, make it effective February 15. Reasons of health."

Lucia didn't try too hard to hide her distaste as she looked at him. "I'm not prepared to wait that long to do something about the letters, Mr. Jenner. I've waited too long as it is."

"Name-calling," he said. "Sticks and stones—"

"It's costing me my job to be called names," she said.

For once Mr. Hasbrouck asserted himself. "No, Lucia, it's not right that it should," he said. "I don't like this business of resigning one bit. Anonymous letters, after all. I don't want to lose you, not with the good reports I've been getting on the way you're taking hold of your new job. Naturally, you don't want to let this thing go on and neither do we. But your resignation isn't the answer."

Mr. Jenner sent him a coldly questioning glance. "What've you got in mind, Dick?"

"Well, I think we should show some backbone over this, Claude. Lucia's been with us over four years, she's done very well and we know she's a fine girl. We aren't going to feel very proud of ourselves if we let her resign over a few anonymous letters from some crackpot. Must be a crackpot, since she doesn't know who it is."

The bank president achieved dignity and decison as he spoke. Lucia, blinking back tears, looked at him with heartfelt gratitude.

The board chairman grunted noncommittally and then

said, "Police aren't the ones to go to, Dick. Lot of flannel mouths on the force, have it all over town. It's a job for the postal authorities. Dunston, I guess. She can find out who to see at the post office here." His gaze switched to Lucia. "But don't spill your business to them, Miss Ruyter. Just ask them who you should see in Dunston. Go to the top man. That's the way to get things done."

"I wish you'd talk it over with your mother first, Lucia," Mr. Hasbrouck inserted. "Why don't you go home tomorrow for the week end and tell her about it? I think she has a right to know before you take it up with the post office people."

Lucia shook her head. "I can't do that, Mr. Hasbrouck. It would worry her terribly. She'd want me to give up my job right away and come home. I don't want that. I want to find out who's doing this to me and why."

Mr. Jenner's expression indicated that if she gave up her job and went home, he would regard it as a satisfactory way out of the dilemma. It moved her to add, "But before I do anything, I'd like to write out my resignation effective at your convenience. I'll leave it with you, you can talk it over with Mr. Jenner and act on it in whatever way seems best to both of you."

The bank president protested. Mr. Jenner gave her a glance that held grudging respect. Lucia took a sheet of paper, dated it with today's date, wrote, "Dear Mr. Hasbrouck: I hereby submit my resignation to be acted on at your convenience," signed her name, and handed it to him across the desk. She said, "May I take the rest of the day off, Mr. Hasbrouck? I'd like to get started on this without any further delay."

"Certainly, Lucia, take whatever time you need."

"Thank you. Would you mind if I took along the letter you got today?"

"Not at all." He gave it to her. "The others—Mr. Jenner turned his over to me—are home if you need

34

them. I wish, though, that you'd talk this over with your mother first."

"We'll see," Lucia temporized. "This may, after all, be cleaned up soon, Mr. Hasbrouck."

"Well, I hope so," the bank president said fervently.

Mr. Jenner said, "Don't forget now, Dunston's the place to deal with, Miss Ruyter. Say as little as possible to the postmaster here. These town officials with their twopenny jobs are all alike when it comes to broadcasting whatever they hear. Bunch of old women, that's what they are."

Lucia offered no comment on this pronouncement. She said thank you and left, and as she closed the door after her heard Mr. Jenner's voice rise in querulous complaint.

He cast a long shadow, she knew. Her job was not safe in spite of what Mr. Hasbrouck had said about their standing in back of her. He could venture only just so far in her defense. If she lost her job—but it was no use worrying about that yet, or the time lapse that might occur before she found another one nearly as good, or what the loss of the financial help she gave her mother would mean to the latter, who'd had to be so careful with money since Lucia's father died.

Chapter Four

Lucia went home and straight to her bedroom closet for the letters, a tall girl with dark hair worn in a knot on the back of her head, eyes more hazel than brown, a mouth whose gentle curve had firmed into a straight line at the moment.

She put the letters in her leather shoulder bag with the one Mr. Hasbrouck had turned over to her and went back to her car.

She had met Mr. Florian, the postmaster. He reminded her a little of her father. He shouldn't be hard to talk to, she encouraged herself on the way to the post office.

But when she entered the building and knocked on the postmaster's door, the voice that called "Come in," didn't sound like Mr. Florian's.

Lucia opened the door and crossed the threshold into a smallish room where two desks, filing cabinets, and an extra chair or two took up most of the space.

The man who stood up from one of the desks looked familiar. Years younger than the postmaster, good looking, he smiled at her, smoothing down rumpled brown hair with a quick swipe of his hand.

"I'd like to see Mr. Florian," Lucia said.

"I'm sorry but he's not here. In fact, he won't be here

for several weeks. He's in Florida recuperating from an operation. I'm Rod Harrison, the assistant postmaster. Can I help you?"

Lucia recognized him now. She had seen him at the bank from time to time and had once asked who he was. She eyed him in doubt. Mr. Jenner had told her to go to the top, to the postal authorities in Dunston. It sounded simple enough when he said it—but who were they exactly? And would Rod Harrison arrange for her to see them without asking why she wanted to?

He saw the distress and indecision written on her face. Drawing a chair up closer to his desk, he said, "Won't you sit down, Miss—uh—?"

"Ruyter." Lucia sat down and so committed herself to relating at least some part of her problem to the young assistant postmaster, who wasn't, after all, quite so young as he'd seemed at first glance. His face had a look of maturity, she thought; he must be past thirty.

He sat down at his desk and asked, "Now what can I do for you, Miss Ruyter?"

"Well, I—" She broke off, started afresh. "In the last couple of weeks I've received two anonymous letters through the mail. Mr. Hasbrouck at the bank—that's where I work—has received three of them full of vicious lies about me. . . ."

Lucia's voice lost its high, tense note as she talked. She settled down a little, his sympathetic attention leading her to say more than she had intended, and much more than would have met with Mr. Jenner's approval. She did not, however, mention Mr. Jenner's attitude toward her or the letter of resignation she had given Mr. Hasbrouck.

At the end she said, "Mr. Jenner thought I should come here, that the postal authorities should be able to put a stop to this thing."

"Well, we'll certainly try," the young assistant postmaster said. "May I see the letters?"

Lucia's bag lay in her lap. Her hand went out instinctively and closed tight on the clasp. She couldn't let him see the letters, not hers, not Mr. Hasbrouck's that called her a tramp. She said, "I'm sorry, Mr. Harrison, but I'd rather you didn't read them. They're awful."

"The point is," he said matter-of-factly, "I'd like to make sure myself that they're a violation of the postal laws."

"Oh, they are," she assured him swiftly. "Perfectly—well, perfectly vile."

He assessed her embarrassment. "Obscene, Miss Ruyter?"

"Oh yes. Very much so."

He didn't press the issue of seeing them. Her manner, along with what she said, made it clear that they really were obscene and defamatory, that this wasn't an imaginary or exaggerated complaint with which she had come to harass the post office. He sat back in his chair, bringing to mind what he knew about her. Her name was familiar in the sense that the names of most of the people in town had become familiar to him in the years he had worked at the post office as a clerk, as superintendent of mails, and, since last year, as assistant postmaster.

He had noticed her at the bank, but what more did he know about her? She came from out of town, didn't she? It seemed that she was well liked. He'd never heard a derogatory reference to her made by anyone. Clerks or carriers would supply further information, but that would have to wait. In the meantime, he'd see what else he could find out for himself before he called Postal Inspection.

He gave Lucia a cigarette and took one himself. He asked her a few questions, where she came from, how long she'd been in Fairmount, what her job was at the bank. Lucia answered readily, relieved that he didn't insist on seeing the letters.

She seemed completely open and honest, Rod Harrison thought. And charming.

Presently he reverted to the letters. "Have you ever received any like them before, Miss Ruyter?"

"Oh no. Never. Even after two of them it's hard for me to believe that anyone would write such things to me."

"May I just have a look at the envelopes?"

She opened her bag, made a move as if to take the letters out of the envelopes, glanced at him, found him, he reflected with amusement and a flicker of satisfaction, worthy of trust, and handed her two letters and Mr. Hasbrouck's to him intact.

He placed them side by side on his desk and looked at them. Then he reached for the phone, and on the direct dialing system within a matter of seconds he was through to Postal Inspector David Madden in the Dunston Federal Building.

Lucia listened to his end of the conversation. "Rod Harrison speaking," he said. "Oh, fine. . . . How are you? . . . Good. . . . Look, Inspector, I've got a young lady here, Miss Lucia Ruyter, who's received two obscene letters mailed here in Fairmount. Her boss, she tells me, has received three of them, defamatory in what they say about her. She has one of his with her and it has a Fairmount postmark too. The first one sent to her was mailed on Monday, January 13, canceled 7 P.M., the second January 23—a week ago today—6:30 P.M. cancellation. The one to her boss was mailed yesterday, 7 P.M. cancellation. . . . No, she says she has no idea. . . . No, I haven't. . . . Well, for various reasons. . . . I thought I'd better leave that up to you. . . . Yes, I'm sure."

Rod Harrison's gaze rested on Lucia as he said this. She looked away, knowing that the inspector had asked if he'd read the letters, and why not, and then if he was sure the complaint was a valid one.

40

At the moment it occurred to her that the young assistant postmaster was showing her much consideration in his handling of the matter.

He said next, "Typewritten. Envelopes look like dime-store stuff.... Wait a minute and I'll ask her.... Miss Ruyter, Inspector Madden says he'll be out this way tomorrow afternoon. Will you be home if he stops by around four-thirty?"

"Yes, that will be fine."

"What's the number on Hunter Street?"

"Twenty-three."

Rod repeated it to the inspector and added directions for finding it. Then, after an interval of listening, he said, "Yes, I'll be here. Okay, Inspector, and thanks a lot."

He hung up, handed the letters back to Lucia, and said, "Well, that takes care of it, I guess. Tomorrow afternoon at four-thirty, Miss Ruyter."

"Thank you very much." Lucia started to rise, but Rod, making conversation to prolong her stay, remarked, "I know you're going to find the inspector very easy to talk to."

"He'll have to see the letters, won't he?"

"Yes, but don't worry about it. They're all in the day's work to him. He's seen plenty like them in his time."

Lucia wasn't reassured. Thinking of the unknown inspector who would read the letters tomorrow, she looked as if she wished she hadn't come near the post office. Her voice weighted with her misgivings, she said, "I hope there won't be any publicity on this."

"Postal inspectors don't go in for publicity," he told her. "They try to protect the innocent parties in an investigation as much as they can."

"Well, that's good." She gave him a troubled smile. "I didn't even know they were the people to go to."

"Oh." He smiled back at her. "That goes to show how quietly they work, doesn't it?"

"Yes, I suppose so." She stood up to leave. "Thank you, Mr. Harrison."

"You're very welcome." He walked to the door with her. "I'll keep in touch with you. This concerns us here, you know. The letters were mailed in town and went through this post office. We'd like to help in any way we can."

But nothing he said lifted the cloud from Lucia's face. After she said good-by and left, he stood in the doorway and watched her walk away, approving of the way she carried her height, the composure she achieved in greeting someone she knew in the lobby.

Whatever the letters said about her couldn't be true, he thought suddenly. He knew a nice girl when he met one. Lucia Ruyter was a nice girl.

He turned back to the office, went through it and out another door into the workroom, where he spoke to the superintendent of mails, describing Lucia's letters, asking the superintendent to alert the distributors who sorted the mail and the carrier on her route to watch for them and if one showed up to bring it to him immediately.

It was early days in a poison pen letter case to start putting a cover on Lucia's mail, he knew, but returning to his office he grinned to himself. For her he'd go above and beyond the call of duty. Any time at all.

Chapter Five

Not long before four-thirty the next afternoon Inspector Madden turned into Hunter Street and began to watch the numbers. Twenty-three was midway along the first block, a big gray house with an ell and a two-car garage some distance in back of it. At the front door there were two bells, one marked *Mrs. Robert Aitken*, the other, *L. Ruyter*. He pressed Lucia's and was admitted so promptly that he knew she must have been on the lookout for him.

She smiled diffidently, said, "Inspector Madden?" and led the way into her apartment.

He dropped his hat and coat on a chair, telling her not to bother hanging them up. His dark eyes ranged over the room, noting at once the typewriter, a standard model, on a table near a window. For the rest, he found the room attractive, although most of the furniture had an old-fashioned look which indicated, he thought, that it probably belonged to her landlady. There were touches, however, the bright-jacketed books on the shelves by the fireplace, the modern still life over it, the gay print in the draperies and slipcovers, that the girl must have added herself.

Lucia eyed him covertly, the tall dark inspector with

his thin face that had a thoughtful, scholarly expression touched with the reserve of one who withheld something of himself from others. It was rather a handsome face, really ,she thought, but, for her purpose, not old enough. He wasn't nearly as old as she would have liked him to be, considering the letters she must give him to read.

"Won't you sit down, Inspector?" She sat down herself on the sofa facing the chair she indicated.

Madden sat down, sorting out his first impressions of her. Somewhere around her middle twenties, appealing, simply dressed in a sweater and skirt, ill at ease at the moment but with poise and breeding that made her try hard to conceal it. She looked, he thought in a conclusion that matched Rod Harrison's, like a nice girl.

Making conversation, Lucia said, "I told Mr. Harrison that postal inspectors are brand-new to me."

"Are they?" David Madden's smile erased the touch of reserve on his face. "I guess it's our destiny always to be brand-new to people, Miss Ruyter, even though we're the oldest investigative agency in the government."

"Are you? How old?"

"Well, we go all the way back to Benjamin Franklin. That's about as far back as an agency could go."

"I should say it is. I can't understand why people don't hear more about you."

"Perhaps we prefer it the way it is," he suggested.

"Still—everybody hears about the FBI."

"Oh yes," said Madden. "The FBI. . . ." He settled back in his chair. "I noticed there were only two names on the door. This is a big house. Doesn't anyone else live in it?"

Lucia explained the arrangement; that Mrs. Aitken, a widow for many years, hadn't liked being alone as she grew older and so had converted the ell into the apartment Lucia now occupied. "For years Grace Klemme, who worked at the bank, had it," she

44

continued. "Grace and I were close friends, I'd gotten to know Mrs. Aitken through her, so when Grace got married and moved out of town last summer I was lucky enough to inherit the apartment."

"I imagine there were other people at the bank who would have liked it, weren't there?" the inspector inquired, with the thought that perhaps the letters were the work of someone who wanted the apartment and was trying to drive Lucia out of Fairmount.

"Not that I know of," she replied. "There was no competition, it was never for rent in the ordinary way, if that's what you mean. Mrs. Aitken and I just got together on it. I was delighted. I like it much better than the place I used to have."

Dismissing rivalry for the apartment as a motive for the letters, Madden turned his attention to Mrs. Aitken. Lucia told him that she had a daughter and grandchildren in California; that, although past seventy, Mrs. Aitken was in excellent health, socially prominent, active in civic affairs, president of the Garden Club, chairman of the Visiting Nurse Association board, and a member of various other local organizations. Lucia went on to tell him how much she liked the older woman and how well they got on together.

There seemed to be nothing in Lucia's living arrangements that would lead to the letters. The inspector proceeded to questions about her background.

She sketched it in. She came from Lowell, Massachusetts, where her father had been president of a bank until his death two years ago. She'd always planned to work in one herself, but when she'd finished college she had decided she should be in a bank where she'd be on her own. "Although," she interpolated lightly, "I wasn't above having my father pull strings on my behalf. That's how I got a job in the bank here. After that it was up to me."

"And how have you made out?"

"Well, just lately I feel entitled to brag." Lucia laughed at herself a little, and then told him about her recent promotion to assistant treasurer in the Loan and Discount Department. "And it came after only four and a half years too," she added. "That's why I feel like bragging. You should have heard Mr. Hasbrouck being pontifical about how I was the youngest person he'd ever given such a responsible job, and how I must make good in it to justify his confidence in me. And so forth."

A promotion over older heads? This looked like a promising field to Madden. He asked, "Were there many people in the department after the job?"

"Oh dear," said Lucia. "Now I have to confess I was the only person qualified for it. The department is small, you see. The vice-president in charge, the treasurer, three clerks, and me. I was bound to get the promotion. The clerks weren't qualified, weren't interested, for that matter. I took night courses in Dunston for two years in Credit Administration and Loans. That's how I got it."

"What about people in other departments? Didn't any of them resent it?"

Lucia shook her head. "I don't think so. It's the bank's policy to promote within departments whenever possible, so there'd be no reason for anyone else to expect to get it."

To Madden's next question she replied that no one from the bank had taken the night courses in Dunston with her.

He dropped the subject and asked, "May I see the letters now?"

"I'll get them," Lucia said in a small voice and left the room.

He heard her cross the kitchen and go into another room. Then he stood up and went over to take a look at her typewriter. It was an Underwood with elite type, he

46

noted. There were a few books on the table beside it, but no paper or envelopes were in sight. He glanced at the books. *Credit Administration*, *Fundamentals of Banking*, *Intallment Loans*—they were hardly titles you'd expect to find in an attractive young woman's apartment, he reflected with a smile. It seemed that she had earned her promotion at the bank.

Lucia came back with the letters. Her eyes averted from his, she handed them to him. "I made coffee," she said. "I'll get it while you're reading those things," and escaped from the room.

Madden sat down with them. He looked at the envelopes first, the neat errorless typing in pica type of Lucia's name and address on two of them and Mr. Hasbrouck's on the third, the 6:30 and 7 P.M. postmarks. The envelopes themselves would be of no value in tracing the writer. They could be bought in any five-and-ten.

The paper, when he opened the first letter, was more promising. It was of good quality watermarked Old Concord Bond.

He read the letters in chronological order without sharing Lucia's feelings of shock and disbelief over hers. He had read many similar ones. But his mouth puckered with distaste as he read. He was a fastidious man and would never become quite used to them.

He went on to Mr. Hasbrouck's and then read all of them a second time, considering the grammar and good sentence construction, the correct spelling throughout. No semiliterate person had written them. They were the product of someone accustomed to writing letters, to the use of a typewriter, possibly someone with business experience.

The inspector had gotten this far when Lucia returned with a tray. He stood up to help her with it, and there followed the interlude of pouring, of his telling her that he liked a little cream but no sugar. Then he went back to his chair, and Lucia's glance settled on the letters lying on the table beside him.

His eyes followed the direction of hers. He asked if he might take them away with him, and when she said yes put them in the inside pocket of his coat, knowing that she would feel more comfortable if they were out of sight.

"What will you do with them?" she inquired.

"Well, for one thing, I'd like to make a study of them myself." Madden did not add that the letters would then be sent to the Questioned Document Examiner in Washington. She seemed more at ease; he didn't want to embarrass her all over again.

"They're so awful," she said in an undertone. "And not true at all. They're—oh, I don't know what kind of a man would write such—" She broke off, overcome with embarrassment at having to protect her innocence of what the letters said about her.

"They're standard accusations," the inspector told her. "The sort of thing we expect to find in poison pen letters sent to a young woman the writer wants to hurt and humiliate."

"Oh." A note of relief sounded in Lucia's voice. "I thought—well, it's hard to imagine that anyone else ever received letters like them."

"I can't quote figures on how many are written a year, Miss Ruyter, but I can assure you that you're in no way unique," Madden said with a smile.

She smiled back at him. "You're making me feel better. Not quite so alone with it."

He picked up his cup, drank, and said, "You mentioned that a man wrote them. Do you have someone in mind?"

"Oh no. But the things they say—no woman could possibly—"

Madden's thoughts, when she spoke of a man writing the letters, had turned to a case a few years back in which a young woman had rejected a married man's advances and become the victim of a flood of obscene letters and postcards that led to the loss of her job before she went to Madden and lodged a complaint. The man was now serving a sentence in the Federal Prison at Danbury, Connecticut. Thinking of him, Madden had wondered if Lucia had a similar type of suspect ready to be named. But it wasn't going to be that easy, it seemed.

He said, "Of course there's no rule about this sort of thing, Miss Ruyter, but it's been my experience that when poison pen letters are just ordinarily obscene, a man probably wrote them. When they're as filthy as the ones you're getting, the writer is very apt to be a woman."

"Really?" Lucia's eyes widened in astonishment. "Women write . . ." Her voice trailed off, picked up again. "Do you think a woman wrote the letters to me?"

He laughed. "Now you don't expect me to commit myself on that one, do you?" As he said this he thought of how much wider still her eyes would be, how outraged she would be, if he added that he had investigated cases in which women had written obscene letters to themselves. Lucia was making a favorable impression on him, but it wasn't outside the realm of possibility that she had written the letters to herself—although not on the typewriter here in her apartment.

He asked her if she could suggest who might have written them. She had no idea, she said. She'd had no trouble, no quarrel with anyone.

The inspector finished his coffee, declined a second cup. He said, "They don't read like the work of a crackpot who more or less picked you out of the air. Whoever wrote them knows quite a lot about you. That you went to a dance with someone named Jack Morse, for instance."

"Yes, but I didn't go to his apartment with him afterward, Inspector!"

"Even so," Madden said, "the writer knows you've gone out with Morse and—well, who's the other one?"

"Phil Parsons. But we've never," she continued emphatically, "spent any week ends together. Our skiing was done on day trips, perfectly aboveboard, every one of them."

"I'm sure they were," Madden said gently. "But the fact remains that the writer knows you go on them."

She'd just about die, Lucia thought, sitting here denying what the letters said about her. She had to, though, she owed it to her self-respect. Her voice shook a little as she said, "None of the things are true."

The postal inspector eyed her sympathetically. She wasn't ready yet to concentrate on the point he was trying to make, but that was understandable. When people received poison pen letters they had to be allowed time to deny the accusations made, be assured and reassured that he didn't believe they were true. It would never do for him to say that the accusations were none of his business anyway; that, whether they were true or not, his business was to prevent the mails being used to send them.

He felt sorry for Lucia, who looked so acutely miserable.

But when he brought her at last to the main point she could only maintain that she had no name to give him. "I'm finding it hard to believe that I actually know anyone who'd write letters like that," she added with a forlorn little smile.

Madden went on leisurely. "By the way, have you received any anonymous phone calls? Sometimes they're tied in with these cases."

Lucia said no, she hadn't, and he continued, "Well then, even though you can't think of anyone with a grievance against you, real or fancied, let's take it from that angle and explore some of the possibilities. A man, say, that you're turned down."

"Heavens," she said, trying to joke. "You make it sound as if they're all over the place."

"Well, are they?"

"Of course not."

"There must be some."

"One or two. Not recent, though."

"How far back?"

She made a face. "Oh well . . . if you must know, Inspector, the two that come first to my mind certainly aren't carrying a torch for me. In fact, one of them, who doesn't even live in Fairmount, has already married someone else. The other's been working in Seattle the past few months."

Madden questioned her about other men she'd gone out with. She could recall nothing that had happened that would lead one of them to harbor resentment toward her.

Men she worked with at the bank? There weren't many unmarried men, and with the few there were she preferred to keep her relationship on a friendly but impersonal basis.

Advances from the married men? Lucia laughed and said that Mr. Hasbrouck, the president, would never allow that sort of thing to go on and neither would Mr. Jenner. She'd met with none of it.

"No reason at all, then, for a wife to get jealous," Madden commented.

"None," Lucia replied firmly.

He studied her in silence for a moment. He didn't feel that she was consciously withholding information; and yet nothing she said gave him the starting point he needed.

When a lull came in his questions Lucia explained that she'd like to keep the bank out of what was, after all, her own personal problem, and then said, "You won't have to talk to Mr. Hasbrouck or Mr. Jenner about this, will you?"

Although Madden was far from convinced that the bank could be kept out of it, he replied, "Not right away. We'll see what develops."

He took out the letters and checked the names again. There were three, Jack Morse, Phil Parsons, Roger Acres.

Phil Parsons, from what Lucia told him, wasn't a promising suspect. He'd been working in Fairmount for the past year but he came from Ohio and had a girl back home. Lucia and he shared a liking for bowling and skiing, and they'd done these things together a few times. That was all there was to their acquaintance.

Who might have seen them together? Anyone. They'd gone skiing at Fall Hill just outside of town and bowled at the Fairmount Bowling Center.

Roger Acres? Lucia and he hadn't been the least bit serious about each other. Roger had been transferred to the Rochester office of his firm before Thanksgiving and had been back in town only once since then, and that was early in December a couple of weeks after he left.

Jack Morse, who figured most prominently in the letters, she dated once or twice a week, she said. She'd met him last fall. They had fun together, liked each other, and that was as far as it went. He'd shown no inclination to get serious about her and wasn't the least bit jealous or demanding in his attitude. He lived in Dunston, worked in an insurance office there, and had no associations with Fairmount that she knew of except through her.

Madden would have inquiries made about Jack Morse in Dunston. But from what Lucia said, he was no more promising a suspect than either of the other young men named in the letters.

He went back to Lucia's job, the bank's customers, her fellow-employees, probing for some seemingly trivial unpleasantness, for undercurrents of hostility, for forgotten quarrels or new ones, for anything at all that stood out from the daily routine.

The girl could think of nothing. The general atmosphere at the bank? Well, there was no more than the normal amount of gossip and feuding that you'd find anywhere. She managed to stay pretty well out of it herself; she found the people she worked with a good bunch.

Jealousy of her outside the bank? Oh no. "I'm not," she added, "outstandingly popular or brilliant or accomplished in any way that would make anyone have it in for me."

No, she replied to his next question, she didn't go out with anyone she was particularly interested in. She had while she was in college, but that was long ago and she'd lost all track of the young man. "I'm quite sure we can leave him out of the picture," she said with a smile.

"We seem to be leaving everybody out of it," Madden remarked. "Everybody, that is, except casual acquaintances. It won't do, Miss Ruyter. The letters are from someone close enough to keep tabs on you."

"I know." She gave him a direct look that carried conviction. "But I don't have the faintest idea who it could be."

Madden let this go to try a new approach. What clubs, he inquired, did she belong to?

None, she told him. She wasn't much interested in them. She'd been asked to join the Junior Woman's Club, but while she hadn't definitely said no, she didn't expect to say yes.

What church? The Methodist. But she wasn't active in it, she went sometimes on Sunday, but not to any of its social affairs. No, she'd never sung in the choir or taught in the Sunday school. She looked rueful at this point and said, "I sound so self-centered, don't I? I guess I never sat down before to consider how little I do that's useful outside my job. But, you see, I was going to school two nights a week for the last two years with lots of studying besides, and this year I'm just enjoying not being tied to all that extra work."

"Of course you are," Madden said. "And, as far as I'm concerned, it suits me fine, cuts down the field of investigation. Think how daunting it would be if you belonged to a lot of clubs and committees and things. I'd have to follow up on all of them."

Lucia laughed. "Well, I'm glad my lack of public spirit does someone some good." Her face sobered, she stirred restlessly. "In another way, though, I don't like such a limited field."

"The bank, your friends, you mean?"

"Yes."

He smiled encouragingly. "Let's try to broaden it a little then. New people you've met, trips you've taken, new contacts you've made, even salesmen, say, coming to the house. Anything at all, in fact, that's a bit different from the usual for you."

"Oh." Lucia eyed him questioningly. "How far back?"

"Well, let's go back three or four weeks for a start. Around the first of the year will do."

"I went home for Christmas and New Year's," Lucia said. "About the only thing I've done since was to go to North Conway the week end after New Year's to ski. But that was with some people from up home. No one from around here was with us."

"Did you meet anyone from around here at North Conway that week end?" Madden inquired.

"Not a soul. But I mentioned that I'd gone to a number of people."

"What about changes at the bank? Anyone new started to work there lately?"

Lucia raised her head, lowered in thought, and looked

54

at him from under her brows. "You keep getting back to the bank, don't you?"

"A good part of your life centers around it," he reminded her.

She sighed and the told him that there had been no changes in the bank personnel for months.

Madden took her day by day through the past month. But she could think of nothing out of the ordinary that had happened to her, nothing that might account for the letters.

It was five-thirty by this time. A knock came on the door. Lucia opened it, admitted Mrs. Aitken, and introduced the postal inspector to her landlady as Mr. Madden.

Mrs. Aitken wouldn't sit down. She was driving out in the country to a friend's for dinner, she said, and had just stopped by to ask Lucia to let the cat in if she heard it crying.

Lucia said she would, Mrs. Aitken chatted a minute longer, and left.

The inspector couldn't miss the good feeling that existed between the older woman and her young tenant. He wasn't disposed to consider Mrs. Aitken seriously as a suspect, but after her departure he asked if she owned a typewriter.

"Mrs. Aitken? Why, she'd never—" Lucia checked herself and a moment later said, "She has no typewriter and doesn't even know how to use one." She came to a full stop before she added, "This is going to be pretty horrible, Inspector, if I have to start suspecting everyone I know who owns a typewriter."

"Don't do that," he said. "At least wait until we find out what kind of a typewriter we're looking for. Otherwise, you'll just make yourself miserable."

"How will you find out?"

"Through our lab in Washington."

"Oh lord, then they'll see the letters too."

"They get them every day in the week, Miss Ruyter They won't think anything of it."

Lucia looked unconvinced. She looked as if she wanted to demand them back. He made haste to take out his fountain pen and handed it to her with the letters, saying "Will you initial them for me, please, with today's date?"

"Why?"

"In case it's necessary for you to identify them later on." He didn't add that this might be in court. He'd ask her to cross that bridge, he reflected, when they came to it.

As it was, Lucia's face took on a doubtful expression. But without further comment she initialed the letters and gave them back to him.

He put them in his pocket and picked up his hat and coat. "Will you let me know right away if there are any more of them?" he asked. "You can reach me or leave a message at this number." He brought out one of his business cards with his office telephone number on it. As he handed it to her, he added, "Can you get me the other letters?"

"Yes, I think so."

"Well, I'd appreciate it if you'd put them in the mail for me as soon as possible."

"I'll try to send them to you Monday."

"That'll be fine." Madden continued, "Don't talk about this to anyone, but keep your eyes and ears open, Miss Ruyter. For all you know, someone else at the bank is getting the same kind of mail. How is it distributed there? Could you get a look at it?"

Lucia thought she could. One of the tellers picked it up every morning, she might be able to get a look at it while the switchboard operator was sorting it.

"Well, see what you can do," he said. "You'll be hearing from me, but in the meantime try not to let this get you down." His warm smile offered encouragement. "Keep telling yourself that you're fighting back now."

Lucia returned his smile. "Thank you, I'll try your prescription, Inspector."

Madden left, heading for the post office to talk the case over with Rod Harrison. Lucia gathered up the coffee cups, carried the tray out to the kitchen, and opened the refrigerator to investigate what it had to offer for dinner.

Later that evening Rod Harrison phoned her. He said he'd called to ask if she felt better now that she'd seen Inspector Madden; but somehow the conversation moved on to other things and lasted almost an hour.

Getting ready for bed, Lucia found herself thinking more about the assistant postmaster than the letters that had brought about their acquaintance.

Chapter Six

Monday morning Lucia engaged the switchboard operator in conversation while she sorted the mail and kept an eye out for letters that resembled the ones sent to her. But there was none.

Later that morning she had a talk with Mr. Hasbrouck. He had anticipated her request for the other letters and had brought them with him from home to give to her.

Lucia thanked him. "I'll mail them to Inspector Madden right away," she said, and went on to tell Mr. Hasbrouck about her interview with the postal inspector.

Mr. Hasbrouck looked a little disappointed when she finished. "I guess I expected too much," he said.

"An overnight solution?" Lucia felt moved to defend Madden. "It's not his fault that I couldn't get him off to a flying start with a whole list of suspects."

"No, it isn't. But I can't understand why you aren't able—" the bank president broke off. They had been through all that before.

There were no letters until Thursday's mail brought one to Mr. Hasbrouck at the bank. Lucia spotted it while the mail was being sorted and so was prepared for Mr. Hasbrouck's phone call a few minutes later.

He handed it to her. "You'll want this for the inspector."

She sighed and slipped it in the pocket of her dress. "Another hymn of hate, Mr. Hasbrouck?"

"That's what it is all right. A little more violent in tone about why I keep a girl like you working here." He paused. "I don't think there's much point in your reading it, Lucia."

"I don't want to."

"Have you thought over what I said about telling your mother?"

Lucia shot an inquiring glance at him from under her brows. Mr. Hasbrouck knew, she'd made it plain enough, that if she told her mother she'd insist that she give up her job and come home. Was he trying to ease her out gracefully?

Not fair to think that. He was being very decent really.

Lucia waited until she got home that afternoon to call David Madden. He wasn't in when she called but was expected soon. She left her name and phone number and turned to household chores while she waited to hear from him.

Presently the phone rang but it wasn't the postal inspector, it was Rod Harrison, who said, "I thought I'd let you know, Miss Ruyter, that you've got another letter. At least it looks like one of them. It turned up in the afternoon collection."

"Oh." Her voice diminished at the prospect. A moment later she said, "Mr. Hasbrouck got one too. I called the inspector about it and now I'm waiting for him to call me back. If he calls before the post office closes, would it be all right for me to pick up the letter tonight to see what it is?"

"Why don't I drop it off on my way home?" Rod suggested. "Wouldn't that be simpler?"

"Why, yes, if you don't mind doing it."

"Not at all. I'd better get off the phone now so the inspector can call you. See you later, Miss Ruyter."

"Yes, and thanks very much." Lucia hung up and presently moved to a window to look out into the winter twilight. Her disquiet grew by the minute. She wished Madden would call.

The man next door drove into his yard and waved to Lucia as he got out of his car. She waved back, her eyes followig him until he went into his house and closed the door.

He and his wife were the nicest couple, she reflected. She'd gotten to know them rather well since she'd moved here—but not so well that either of them knew enough about her to write the letters.

She sighed impatiently at the turn her thoughts, involuntarily had taken. Her neighbors, of all people. What earthly reason would they have for doing it?

Who had a reason, though? No one she could think of, not a single person.

The telephone rang. She rushed to answer it, and this time Madden was on the line. It was a relief to hear his quiet voice, the mere sound of it conveyed a promise of help to her.

She told him about Mr. Hasbrouck's letter and the one Rod was going to bring her.

"He'll drop it off on his way home?"

"Yes."

Madden didn't miss the tremor in her voice. Poor girl, he thought. They're getting her down.

What Rod had told him about Lucia had strengthened his own favorable impression of her. He no longer felt it necessary to keep in mind the possibility that she was writing the letters herself. She was too stable a person to do it.

His thoughts went to his own plans. He wouldn't be able to go to Fairmount tomorrow. If he were going at all this week, it would have to be tonight.

He asked Lucia if she'd be home that evening, and when she said yes told her he would be out to see her around eight o'clock.

Lucia hung up and started for the kitchen to prepare dinner. Then the doorbell rang and she admitted Rod Harrison.

The letter he handed her was much like its predecessors and worded in much the same language. But, with Rod in the room while she read it, it seemed worse. She didn't look at him as she said, "It's the same as the others."

"Oh, too bad." His blue eyes revealed his concern for her. "It doesn't say anything that points to who wrote it?"

"Not a thing." Lucia replaced the letter in its envelope.

"I hope the inspector can clear it up fast," Rod said. "It's pretty rough to put up with."

"Oh well." Lucia managed a smile. "I think what I need right now is a drink. Maybe a martini. Would you like one, Mr. Harrison?"

"I sure would," he replied, knowing very well that it would make him late for dinner and that his married sister, with whom he lived, stressed punctuality at table. But there was one small matter that needed to be cleared up with Lucia, and he proceeded to take care of it. "Why the Mr. Harrison?" he said. "Everyone else calls me Rod. I don't see why you shouldn't."

"All right, I'll call you Rod too." Lucia gave him another smile and got to her feet. "Now let's see about the martinis."

He followed her into the kitchen. "Not that I'm going to help," he said. "I'll just lend moral support."

He lounged against a cupboard while she made the drinks and nodded approval when he tasted his. "Good girl," he said. "It's not every woman who can pass on loans at a bank and make a good martini too."

She raised an eyebrow. "Who told you what department I work in?"

"Never mind. At the post office we have our own ways of finding out things."

They took their drinks back to the living room. When they had finished them and the refills in the pitcher, Rod said he must go. He was late for dinner, he was holding up hers, and she had the inspector coming.

But in spite of what he said he seemed reluctant to leave. Lingering at the door, he asked if she'd go to the ice show at the Dunston arena with him tomorrow night.

Lucia said she'd like very much to go. When Rod left after arranging what time he was to call for her the next night, she felt lighthearted indeed as she began to put together a hit-or-miss dinner. Rod was so attractive, she told herself. And so nice.

She thought over the items of information he had given her about himself while they were drinking their martinis. A girl hadn't been mentioned, wouldn't have been, of course, but it seemed safe to assume that he didn't have one or he'd be dating her, not Lucia, for the ice show tomorrow night.

Lucia's eyes were bright her cheeks pink with thoughts of him. She didn't look at all like the victim of a poison pen writer as she sat down to her dinner. At the moment there was no room in her mind for the letters.

Inspector Madden's arrival turned her attention back to them. She handed him the latest one and didn't try to find an excuse to remove herself from the room while he read it. I'm getting used to them, she reflected in wonderment. Actually used to them.

The postal inspector read it, a wry expression on his thin dark face. Then he studied it, the same block style, good grammar and spelling, as the others, the same watermarked paper and dime-store envelope. Jack Morse

63

was named in it and a man named Tony White.

Presently Madden laid it aside and inquired. "Who's Tony White?"

"He works at the bank." Lucia's reply came less calmly than she intended, as she recalled what the letter said about her relationship with Tony White. She added swiftly, "I've never had a date with him in my life. The letter, I know, refers to my dancing with him at the Black Lantern Inn. But that was at the bank's Christmas party. And I danced with other people besides Tony."

"Is he married or single?" Madden's thoughts were divided between a jealous wife and a jealous girl friend.

"Single. But, no one I'd care to go out with. He thinks he's God's gift to women. It just happened that I danced with him a few times that night."

"Who was at the Christmas party besides the employees?"

"No one else. Of course there were other people at the Black Lantern that night who could have seen me dancing with Tony."

"Anyone from Fairmount that you noticed?"

"Not that I recall. But you know how people talk. After the party there must have been discussion of who danced with this one or that one and who drank too much and so on."

Madden could understand Lucia's reluctance to believe that the letters were being written by someone with whom she worked every day at the bank. But he didn't share her tendency to look for an outsider.

He asked to see Mr. Hasbrouck's letter, had her initial and date both of them, and put them in his pocket.

Lucia had lit a fire in the fireplace just before the inspector's arrival. His gaze on the leaping flames, he began, "I know you'd like to keep the bank out of this, Miss Ruyter, but it just can't be done. It looks to me as if someone connected with it is writing the letters."

Lucia looked at him with resignation. "All right. Where shall we start? With Mr. Ingalls, the vice-president in charge of my department?"

"We might as well start with him as anywhere." Madden's tone and smile were relaxed. The pleasant room with its homelike touches and the open fire were conducive to relaxation. Lucia added one more ingredient to it by remarking, "I'll make us a drink first. Scotch and soda, if that will suit you, Inspector."

"It will suit me fine, thank you."

After she left the room Madden stretched out in the deep chair and, instead of thinking about his case, let his thoughts drift to winter evenings in the past when he and Estelle had sat with drinks in front of a fire sometimes talking, sometimes listening to records. She had liked many of the moderns, but Beethoven had been her favorite. He would never hear *Eroica* without thinking of her. . . .

The memory, the ghost of pain rather than pain itself, stirred in David Madden as he thought of his dead wife. It was part of the past now, the first shock and anguish of the doctor's words, the futile operation, the hospital room where he had watched his wife die a little, day by day until, a shell of herself, she gave up the struggle and went away in her sleep while he sat beside her, her hand in his. He had thought himself prepared for her death. But when it came he had learned that there was no such thing as being prepared for the death of the person you loved best in the world. At first it had seemed like the end of everything, the pain and loss unbearable. He'd had no choice though, except to live with it, and had gradually made a new way of life for himself, lonely at times but fairly adequate with the interest he took in his work. He began to pick up old friendships and form new ones. He went out with some of the women his friends produced for him, and now and then became interested in one of them. But these several years later he still hadn't found anyone he wanted to put in Estelle's place.

The ghost of the old pain left him as Lucia came back into the room with their drinks. He took his, ice cubes jostling each other in the glass, and commented smilingly, "I see you don't share the usual feminine habit of stinting on ice, Miss Ruyter. You know, one lonely little cube melting away in a sea of liquid."

"I know." Lucia laughed and settled down opposite him, reflecting that she'd just as soon he and Rod Harrison didn't compare notes on how well she mixed drinks. It wasn't, after all, a particularly ladylike accomplishment.

Madden drank from his glass and then said, "Now let's talk about people at the bank."

For the next hour or more they talked about them, he dissecting her impressions of her fellow-employees, finding out a great deal about the workings of the bank, not finding, in anything she told him, a motive for the letters.

And yet it had to be there, they were somehow missing it. This thought persisted in the postal inspector's mind after he had said good night to Lucia and started back to Dunston. The bank came into the picture, it was time he went there himself. He couldn't go tomorrow but he would would go Monday.

Chapter Seven

The next morning, under the case number assigned to them by Division Headquarters in Boston, Madden sent the two letters Lucia had given him the night before to the Identification Bureau in Washington, numbering them Q-7 and Q-8. He turned over to his investigative aide a list of the men named in them and then left for a town where a case involving the theft of blank money-order forms was coming to an end. The post office clerk responsible for the theft had confessed and been arrested, but there were various points still to be cleared up before Madden could put the case aside until it came to trial. Today should wind it up, he thought, he should be able to leave for Providence tonight to spend the week end with his sister. Monday he'd go to the Fairmount bank.

But early Monday morning his plans were changed by a Dunston police lieutenant, who phoned to tell him that in a case of attempted murder by poison the night before the victim, now in the hospital, said that his violent stomach cramps started after he drank whisky sent to him by mail. The hospital pathologist had just confirmed the presence of arsenic in the whisky.

Madden said, "I'll get right on it," and that was his

day. He went first to the hospital to talk with the victim and then to the police station to take part in the interrogation of a man and woman brought in for questioning after being named as suspects by the victim.

The wrapping paper, twine, and cardboard box in which the whisky had been mailed as an anonymous gift had been found in the victim's house, and other evidence was soon assembled. But it wasn't until evening after an all-day interrogation that a confession was finally obtained from the pair.

When he was on his way home Madden couldn't decide who was the more witless, the victim who drank the anonymous whisky or the would-be murderers, the woman who addressed the package in her own handwriting and the man who tied it with twine cut from a ball the police found in his room. The combined intelligence of all three of them wouldn't add up to one normal I.Q., Madden thought.

But the case was too squalid to dwell on. He dismissed it from his mind until the next morning when he went to the county jail to question the pair again on details of their mailing of the whisky.

By noon he was back at his office, where he found a message from Lucia asking him to call her.

He looked at his watch and then tried her home telephone number on the chance that she had gone home for lunch. She answered the phone and said she had called him because she had spotted three of the letters in the bank's mail that morning.

"Three?" he said. "The writer's been very busy. Who were they to?"

"Mr. Hasbrouck, Mr. Blaine, one of the trust officers, and Lila Ross, a stenographer." Lucia continued, "At first I felt just about sick thinking all of them said things about me. But now I don't think so. I watched while Lila opened hers and she looked stunned at first. Then her face got red as fire and she rushed off to the restroom. Her letter, you see, said something about her. When she came back she didn't have it with her and looked as if she'd been crying."

"Too bad she got rid of it," Madden remarked.

"Yes, but I didn't feel I could follow her into the restroom and try to stop her. I don't know her that well. I felt awfully sorry for her, though."

"Is this girl married?"

"No. She's not exactly a girl either. She's worked at the bank for years and must be past forty."

"Oh. Do you have much contact with her away from the bank?"

"No, I don't see her at all."

"How did Mr. Blaine react to his letter?" Madden asked next.

"I don't know. I can't see him from my desk. I just hope his letter said nothing about me. Mr. Hasbrouck's did, of course. It said that if he didn't get rid of me soon, Mr. Jenner and the other board members would be asked to do it for him." Lucia paused and then said on a subdued note, "If it ever comes to that, I'll just have to get out. It would be too embarrassing all around for me to stay."

"I don't see why. As long as you've got Hasbrouck on your side, you're all right."

"You don't know Mr. Jenner. He wouldn't let Mr. Hasbrouck stay on my side."

"Well, don't worry about that just yet," Madden said. "If other people at the bank start getting letters, it takes some of the weight off you. And, by the way, did Hasbrouck give you the one he got this morning?"

"No. He asked for your address. He said he was going out in a few minutes and he'd mail it to you himself."

"Well, he could have given it to me if he'd waited until this afternoon. I'm planning to see him then. Will you

69

tell him I'm coming?"

Lucia's sigh accepted the inevitable. "I'll tell him," she said.

The postal inspector left for Fairmount after lunch and went to the bank, a red brick building with a parking lot and drive-in window, on a side street a little away from the Center.

Mr. Hasbrouck saw him immediately. Madden had been looking forward to meeting Lucia's defender, who tilted with Mr. Jenner on her behalf. A less knightly figure it would be hard to find, he thought. Plump, partly bald, conservatively dressed, the bank president's appearance suggested the dignity of his position. His florid color suggested high blood pressure. It might well go higher, Madden thought, before this affair was ended. Banks and public confidence went hand in hand; bank officials were apt to get excited if scandal touched their personnel.

Mr. Hasbrouck said he would like to be of assistance in clearing up this unfortunate affair, but that he was at a loss to account for it. Then he talked at some length about what a fine girl Lucia was and the high caliber generally of the bank's personnel.

Madden said when he could get in a word, "Still, the bank seems to be involved in this, Mr. Hasbrouck." Without disclosing that Lucia was the source of his information, he went on to suggest the possibility that Lila Ross and Alec Blaine had also received letters from the poison pen writer.

Mr. Hasbrouck's florid color deepened. This was news to him, he said. He knew nothing about it.

"Their letters only came this morning. They change the focus a bit, don't you think?" The inspector paused to lend emphasis to his next words. "Miss Ross, I understand, is an older woman. It seems to me that the bank would be the one meeting ground she'd have with

Miss Ruyter. You'd know better than I if that also holds true of her and Mr. Blaine."

Madden had made a point. Mr. Hasbrouck fell silent, his babyish mouth pursed in thought. At last he said, "I don't know what other meeting ground Blaine and Miss Ross could have. He's a trust officer, she's a stenographer, but as it happens she doesn't have occasion to take dictation from him or do any work for him that I know of."

"Is Blaine married?"

"Oh yes. Has a son out of college working for some firm in the West. His wife's a charming woman, very active in town affairs. If there's any association between him and Miss Ross, I'm sure it's not the usual sort of thing. Her character's above reproach. She's the sole support of a widowed mother and—uh—well, she's not a young woman, she's—uh—"

Madden helped him out. "No Marilyn Monroe?"

"Indeed not. And I don't know what else there could be that Blaine and she—"

"Perhaps he could tell us himself," Madden suggested.

Mr. Hasbrouck sighed, pressed a buzzer on his desk that summoned his secretary, and told her he wanted to see Mr. Blaine in his office.

Alec Blaine came in unobtrusively. He was the kind of man, Madden thought, who would spend his whole life being unobtrusive, arriving promptly when summoned, in fact, holding himself perpetually in readiness to be summoned by voices that carried more authority than his. He was tallish but not tall, his hair receded a little but not noticeably from a high lined forehead, he was neither fat nor thin, he was middle-aged, but exactly where he fitted into that category it was hard to tell. He had no dominant characteristic, he lacked drive, vitality, any degree of forcefulness. How would he be described on a *Wanted* poster?

71

But a closer study of the newcomer indicated that, for all his neutral appearance, Alec Blaine had a quality of gentleness about him. It was there in the lines of his mouth and in the pale blue eyes he bent on Madden.

Then dismay flitted across his face as the bank president said, "Mr. Blaine . . . Postal Inspector Madden," but he smiled politely, shook hands, and sat down near the inspector after being told by Mr. Hasbrouck to have a seat.

Mr. Hasbrouck said next, "A few people around here seem to be getting anonymous letters lately, Alec. If you've received one—and the inspector tells me you have—he'd like to know about it."

Dismay, this time not fleeting, appeared again on Alec Blaine's face. He said nothing. There was no need to as the bank president continued hastily. "If you have received such a letter, whatever it says will be between you and Inspector Madden. It concerns no one else. And after all, when it's anonymous—" Mr. Hasbrouck's grimace expressed his strong disapproval of such communications, "it's not worth anyone's serious attention."

"No, of course not, Dick," Alec Blaine answered. But his face denied his words, made it plain that he was giving serious attention to his letter. He subsided then, dividing an uncertain glance between Mr. Hasbrouck and Madden.

The latter came to his assistance. "You did receive one of the letters, Mr. Blaine?"

The pale blue eyes settled briefly on Madden's face and turned away. "Yes," he replied. "A letter that said preposterous things. It said—"

"Wait a minute, Alec," Mr. Hasbrouck interposed. "I think it would be better if you and the inspector talked this over without me sitting in on it."

His subordinate shook his head. "I'd rather you stayed, Dick. As a matter of fact, you're my alibi," he smiled feebly, "for what the letter accuses me of. It says that last Wednesday night, the night you and I went to the AIB meeting in Dunston, I was out with Miss Ross. Miss Ross here at the bank. It says I took Miss Ross to my home that night while my wife was out and"—he paused looking flustered—"well, it says in very crude language that we—had intimate relations. . . ." His voice trailed off and threw away the last of this statement.

The inspector asked, "Was your wife out that night, Mr. Blaine?"

"Yes, I believe so. A Visiting Nurse Association meeting. She's on the board, you see." He ran his fingers agitatedly through his sparse lank hair. "But I wasn't with Miss Ross that night or any other night. Mr. Hasbrouck will tell you that last Wednesday night we were at the meeting in Dunston together." His glance sought confirmation from the bank president. "You remember it, Dick."

"Yes, yes, of course. It was close to midnight when we got home."

Madden said, "I'm not questioning your story of where you were that night, Mr. Blaine. The point is, whoever wrote the letter apparently didn't know you'd gone to the meeting in Dunston but did know your wife was out, the house empty."

Alec Blaine relaxed a little. "Oh yes, I see what you mean."

The inspector, thinking aloud, asked, "How many people here at the bank were apt to have known you and Mr. Hasbrouck planned to attend that meeting?"

They consulted together, presently named two vice-presidents and another trust officer who had known. Beyond that they couldn't recall the matter being mentioned to anyone else.

"May I see the letter you received, Mr. Blaine?" Madden asked next.

Alec Blaine's hand went defensively to his breast pocket. "Well . . ." More flustered than ever, he looked at Madden. "The language—I told you it was crude. Actually, it was worse than that. It was—"

Madden replied equably, "I've seen it all at one time or another, Mr. Blaine, in poison pen letters. It won't bother me."

It did, of course, to some extent, when the other man reluctantly handed over the letter. It was written on the now familiar stationery, the typing equally familiar, the language as obscene as that used in Lucia's letters. He finished reading it and said, "Mr. Blaine, as fast as these letters come to my attention I'm forwarding them to our Questioned Document Examiner in Washington. If you don't mind, I'd like to keep this one and send it along too."

Alec Blaine looked acutely unhappy. Madden, guessing that his objection would be the usual one raised to this request, added, "They don't pay any attention to what these letters say at the lab, Mr. Blaine. They're all in the day's work to them, the way deposits and withdrawals are all in the day's work here at the bank."

When Alec Blaine still hesitated Mr. Hasbrouck said, "We've got to co-operate, Alec. Get this thing cleared up as fast as we can."

"Yes, I suppose so. All right, Inspector, you keep the letter." He eyed Madden in sudden alarm. "Does my wife have to know about it?"

"Well, not at the moment. Perhaps later, if the letters keep coming, I'll need to talk to her," Madden replied, making the inference that the other man was a henpecked husband. Then he said, "But since you're in the fortunate position of being able to prove that what the letter says isn't true, don't you think it might be a good idea to talk it over with Mrs. Blaine right away?"

"Perhaps it would be," Alec Blaine said with no

conviction whatsoever in his voice.

Madden had him initial and date the letter and then went on to ask him how well he knew Lila Ross.

He didn't know her socially, didn't see her at all except at the bank, Alec Blaine said. They didn't belong to the same church or clubs or other organizations, she had never been to his house, his wife had only a speaking acquaintance with her.

Further questions brought the reply that he knew of no one who might have written the letters, he'd had no trouble with anyone at the bank. His face took a self-deprecating expression and his glance went to the bank president as he added, "I don't like arguments, Inspector. I do all I can to keep things running smoothly, keep the peace, you might say."

Yes, Madden thought, looking at him, you probably do. Even when it meant sacrificing your pride, your self-respect, your first aim would be to keep the peace.

But, he thought next, more than one man as mild as Alec Blaine had found an outlet for aggressive impulses kept too long under wraps through writing scurrilous letters.

He thanked him for his help and asked him to let him know if he received another letter. Alec Blaine said he would and departed as unobtrusively as he had arrived.

Lila Ross, aging, angular prototype of the spinster taking care of a widowed mother, burst into tears as soon as the matter was broached to her. Mr. Hasbrouck made ineffectual attempts to soothe her, but it was Madden who managed it finally, getting her to understand that she mustn't let her feelings become so intense over something that had been going on since the dawn of history. "And perhaps before," he continued with a smile. "Perhaps some of the symbols carved in caves were poison pen, Miss Ross."

She essayed a dim answering smile to that; and at last she was ready to talk and had nothing to tell, no name to suggest as the author of her letter, no idea of why she was selected as its target. A blameless, pathetically empty life emerged under the postal inspector's questioning. She couldn't produce the letter she had received. "I couldn't bear to have it around," she quavered. "I thought I'd die when I read it. I took it right to the restroom and tore it to bits and—well, I got rid of it."

He showed her Alec Blaine's, not the letter itself, just the envelope.

She nodded, and it seemed she must suffer a stroke from the rush of blood to her face. "So he got one too," she said in a smothered voice. "Oh. . . ."

Madden took pity on her and let her go. Mr. Hasbrouck also took pity on her. "Take the rest of the afternoon off, Miss Ross," he said. "Go straight home and rest and try not to think about it any more."

Madden didn't want that at all. He wanted the victims of the letters to keep thinking about them, to cast around in their minds and bring to him any bits of information that came to the surface. But he expected none from Lila Ross and merely asked her not to destroy it but to send it to him if she received another letter.

She said she would and fled, closing the door after her.

Left alone with the inspector, Mr. Hasbrouck seemed subdued. Lila Ross had brought home to him the anguish the letters could cause and the prospect, more likely than ever, that they were the work of someone employed at the bank.

Madden lit a cigarette and listened while Mr. Hasbrouck deplored the whole situation, saying repeatedly, "We just can't have a thing like this going on. A nice girl like Lucia Ruyter and now Blaine and Miss Ross. We've got to put a stop to it."

Madden agreed that they should. Presently he asked,

"How many typewriters are there in the bank, Mr. Hasbrouck?"

After some thought the older man came up with the estimate of twenty-five. "I can find out the exact number if you want it," he appended.

"What I really want is a sample of the typing from every machine in the bank."

"Yes. Well, I'll try to get them for you quietly. The less talk the better." The banker's forehead creased in a worried frown. "There'll be some talk anyway, I suppose—unless this thing can be cleared up in a hurry." He looked hopefully at Madden. "Do you think there's a chance of that?"

"I don't know. Sometimes these cases are cleared up quickly, sometimes they go on and on."

"Oh." Mr. Hasbrouck's frown deepened. "Well, I'll see what I can do about getting the typing samples for you right away."

"Some of them must be already available," Madden observed. "The officers have their own secretaries, don't they?"

"Well, we don't use that term in banks. Mildred—Mrs. Cummings—is my secretary and works only for me, but the work of the others is more or less divided up. However—" He sorted through papers on his desk and handed two sheets stapled together to Madden. "Here are some notes on a speech Mrs. Cummings typed for me this morning. She made a carbon copy so you may keep that one, Inspector. Her machine is an IBM electric."

Madden made a note of this on the top sheet, had Mr. Hasbrouck initial and date both of them, and put them away with Alec Blaine's letter.

Mr. Hasbrouck proceeded to rummage through his files for other typing samples from various machines, but then it turned out he could make positive identification of none of their makes. "Mrs. Cummings will know," he said. "I'll have her check them and get the rest of the samples. She can do it after everyone's left for the day. She's very obliging about staying overtime."

Madden inquired about Mrs. Cummings, a plump cheerful girl who had ushered him into the banker's office. She'd been married two or three years, had worked for him eight years, Mr. Hasbrouck said. She was a reliable, competent secretary and the soul of discretion.

Madden nodded acceptance of this and then said, "She'll be here until all hours, I'm afraid. It isn't a question of typing the quick brown fox jumped over the lazy dog once or twice on each machine. For a thorough analysis, I'd like two pages from each one, single-spaced like the letters, initialed and dated and marked with the make and model of the typewriter. The sooner I have them, of course the better progress I'll make with the investigation."

Mr. Hasbrouck said he thought Mrs. Cummings would be able to pull many of the samples out of the files; that she would have them ready for him the next afternoon when he would be going through Fairmount on his way back from a neighboring town.

The inspector moved on to the bank personnel. There were, he learned to his surprise, not expecting that there would be so many, seventy-two people employed, ranging from the president through three vice-presidents, two of them also trust officers, assistant vice-presidents, a secretary, treasurer, four assistant treasurers (titles, he reflected at this point, were distributed pretty freely in banks. To compensate for a lesser pay scale than industry?), a cashier, assistant cashier, head teller, operations officer, and so forth all the way down to the custodians. (No vice-president in charge of custodians?)

Mr. McGinley, assistant vice-president and operations officer, Mr. Hasbrouck continued, was in closer touch with the employees than he was. But Mr. McGinley had reported no particular friction recently.

Promotions? Well, a new head teller had been appointed a couple of months ago on the retirement of his predecessor. But he was in line for the job on the basis of tenure of service and ability. It had caused no feeling.

Mr. Hasbrouck went on to assure Madden that rivalries and tensions within the bank were kept at an absolute minimum, that no one could ask for a place to function more smoothly.

Poison pen letters had no existence in this recital, Madden reflected. Also, it held human nature in abeyance.

He brought up next the question of extramarital activities. Mr. Hasbrouck disclaimed the likelihood of a jealous wife or husband authoring the letters. "The employees know better," he said. "They know that if they got mixed up in anything that might lead to a scandal, they just wouldn't be working here any longer. We couldn't have it. Not in a bank."

They were back on public confidence, a bank's position as a public trust. The postal inspector got them off that by asking for specific information on the personnel. The bank president then summoned Mr. McGinley, the operations officer, who supplied Madden with a list that included the name and address of everyone employed at the bank. The operations officer, although more realistic than Mr. Hasbrouck in conceding that there were incidents, more than a minimum amount of friction at times, could suggest nothing recent or outstanding of that nature. No one had been fired or had other reason to bear a grudge.

Soon thereafter Madden took his leave and went to the Fairmount police station where he conferred with the chief on the personnel list. A few names on it were in the police files for traffic violations but that was all. No one had a record that pointed toward authorship of the letters.

Madden went next to the post office with his list. Rod checked it name by name, supplying information about nearly everyone on it. What he said eliminated, on the basis of character and reputation, more than one-third of the list. But beyond that, for lack of fuller knowledge, he wasn't prepared to go. Madden still had forty names left as possible suspects. He asked Rod to put a cover on the bank's mail and went back to Dunston.

There he numbered Alec Blaine's letter Q-9, and the typing sample Mr. Hasbrouck had given him K-1, the first known document he would send to Washington. Tomorrow he would have about twenty-five of them to sort out, samples from every typewriter in the bank.

When the postal inspector had driven into the bank parking lot that afternoon he had missed Inez Blaine driving out of it by only a minute or two.

She had cashed a check at the bank, dispensing smiles and nods as she entered the building and stopping to chat with various people before she went to one of the teller stations.

Calvin Eads, the only teller free at the moment, cashed her check. Inez had no smile for him. From the time he started to work at the bank he had shown immunity to her charm. He'd been brusque, downright rude to her more times than she could count. Today he looked hung over, she thought. He drank like a fish, everyone knew it. But that didn't excuse his surliness as he counted out her money and shoved it at her without even the courtesy of a glance in her direction. He was insufferable, not fit to hold a job that put him in contact with the public.

Ben Davidson came out of Mr. Hasbrouck's office as she left the teller station and gave her a cheery smile and greeting. Inez smiled back at him with a graciousness that was all on the surface. He was pretty cocky these days, she told herself vindictively. If he knew what she knew about him, he wouldn't be so cocky! But no wonder he thought he was all set. From what Alec told her, Ben's promotion to vice-president and public relations officer was only waiting on old Mr. Raeburn's retirement a couple of months from now. Well, Ben had better give his wife a few lessons in public relations. A snob like her, who thought she was so much better than everyone else, could use them.

Inez didn't stop at Alec's desk to speak to him. She had savored his silence and woe-begone expression at lunch. He'd looked like a sick cat, she'd thought, and well he might after the letter he'd gotten this morning. It was just what he'd deserved. He had no pride or self-respect. In spite of the way Lucia had treated Gibb, Alec was back at singing her praises since Inez had begun to draw him out about her. He needed to be brought to heel.

She barely glanced in Lucia's direction as she left the bank. The girl's smooth dark head bent over her work was, in itself, an irritation. That severe hairdo was just an affectation, she told herself. Any other girl with hair as nice as hers would fluff it out, show it off a little. Not Lucia, though. She preferred to pose as the successful career girl with no time for frills. It was simply maddening to think the girl was still there, sitting at her desk in the railed enclosure, in spite of the letters Inez had written about her. What was the matter with Dick Hasbrouck?—and that dithering old fool Jenner who prided himself on his toughness? How much longer were they going to permit Lucia to stay on?

Well, until they did something about her, Inez would keep on writing the letters. If that wasn't enough—but she needn't think right now about what she'd do if it wasn't.

On the front steps she met Fred Bauer, the treasurer.

She had no smile for him, he none for her. They'd clashed at the special town meeting on the new school three weeks ago. Fred, swollen with self-importance, had been very sarcastic and insulting to Inez, not for the first time either. He thought he was God Almighty since he'd been made chairman of the school board.

Fred Bauer gave her a curt nod as he passed her. Inez turned and gave him a speculative look. Then, deep in thought, she went down the steps and around the corner of the building to the parking lot.

By the time she reached her car she knew what she was going to do, and had already discounted the possibility that scattering her shot a little might deflect it from Lucia, her main target. She'd do it just once; the opportunity to pay back a few scores was too irresistible to miss.

Driving out of the parking lot, Inez reveled in a sudden, heady sense of power.

Chapter Eight

Two days later another letter was sent to Lucia. Rod told her about it on the phone and said he would drop it off on his way home. "I wish you wouldn't read it, though," he added. "Why don't you just turn it over to Madden unopened?"

"I should but I probably won't," she said dejectedly. "I can't bear to read them, and yet I can't leave them unopened."

Rod didn't fail to catch the dejected note in her voice. He said, "Well, if you must read it, how about having dinner with me afterward?"

"A shoulder to cry on?"

"Whenever you want to use it," he assured her. "I'll drop off the letter, go home and wash up, and then pick you up. That okay?"

"Fine. But wouldn't it be easier for you to take the letter home and give it to me later?"

"You want me to lose my job, woman, taking home letters that aren't addressed to me?"

"Oh. Regulations?"

"That's right, regulations. I'll drop it off."

Rod had been nearly ready to leave for the day when one of the distributors sorting mail turned Lucia's letter over to him. A few minutes after his phone call he arrived to deliver it to her. He was slow, however, to take it out of his pocket, and told her again that he wished she'd turn it over unopened to Madden. "Why read such stuff?" he demanded.

"I said I couldn't help it, didn't I?" Lucia held out her hand for it. "My regular dose of poison."

This time it had a different flavor. After its accusations about her relations with men it said: "You'd better be careful or you'll get what's coming to you one of these days. You should have gotten it long ago. Just read some of the cases in the newspapers about what happens to girls like you. If you don't take warning from them and mend your ways, it will be too late."

"Well," Lucia said, and read this paragraph aloud to Rod.

"That's a hell of a thing!" he exclaimed. "I don't like it one bit."

"It's just meant to scare me." Lucia kept her voice light. "And after all, since I'm not leading the kind of life the letters accuse me of, I won't be putting myself in a situation where I might get beaten up or strangled some night. So actually it doesn't mean much."

She talked on in that vein, wanting to convince herself as well as Rod that the new note needn't be taken seriously. She was more successful with herself than with Rod. His anxiety was still apparent when he left.

Lucia repeated much the same things to David Madden who made an unexpected appearance soon after Rod's departure.

The postal inspector, unable to get to Fairmount the day before, had been late that day in arriving at the bank to collect the bulky pile of typing samples Mr. Hasbrouck had ready. The latter had waited for him, though, after everyone else had left, and been prepared to talk at considerable length about the bank personnel. But at the end of their discussion Madden was no wiser than at the start of it, and then decided to drop in on Lucia to see if she had any fresh ideas or information to offer.

She gave him the letter. He read it and listened to what she said about how meaningless its threatening note was.

"When you get right down to it," she concluded, "it's on a par with my mother's warning when I was a child. 'Be careful crossing the street now, if you aren't, you might get hit by a car.' . . . Oh dear." She looked rueful suddenly. "That's not a good comparison for me to make. I did get hit by a car, you see, one night last November. A hit-and-run driver."

"A hit-and-run driver?" Madden was at once alert. "How'd it happen?"

She told him about it and then said, "The police thought, the way it was raining, that the driver might not even have realized he'd hit me." After a pause she added, "I don't believe that, I'm not all that charitable. I know I screamed like mad as I jumped back, and with the headlights right on me it doesn't seem possible the driver didn't see me."

"Is the coffee shop you went to right in the Center?"

"No, it's only three or four blocks from here in a residential neighborhood where small businesses have come in. There were trees, though," Lucia made an effort to be fair, "and I was wearing a dark raincoat—I've bought a light one since—and if the driver didn't see me I suppose he could have been deaf or something and didn't hear me scream."

Madden's interest in the accident persisted. "Are you using 'he' in the general sense, Miss Ruyter, or did you get the impression the driver was a man?"

"Heavens no. I got no impression at all. Just a light car—I don't know how big it really was but it looked enormous to me—tearing around the corner and on top of me before I knew it was coming."

"Were you on the right or left of it as it came toward you?"

"On the left, the driver's side. Which makes it still less likely that I wasn't seen at all." Lucia spoke dryly. "It was a hit-and-run, all right."

Madden fell silent, turning the accident over in his mind. Last November was three months ago. He could find no connection between the hit-and-run case and the outbreak of poison pen letters, except that Lucia was involved in both. He carried this point a step farther. Lucia might have been seriously injured or killed in the accident; today's letter implied that her allegedly immoral behavior could lead to serious injury or death for her.

He didn't like it. It might well be a farfetched train of thought, he told himself, but it was a disturbing one.

He reread the last paragraph of the letter. It brought the possibility of a rejected suitor into the foreground again. His aide had investigated the three young men whose names appeared in Lucia's letters and reported that they seemed to be in the clear. But they weren't the only young men the girl knew.

Madden asked for more names, particularly the men she'd gone out with since last summer.

It turned into a memory exercise for Lucia. But names came out, and even when she protested that someone was a mere acquaintance Madden wrote the name down.

There were quite a few names before they were done, Lucia being more popular than she was prepared to admit. No reason she shouldn't be, Madden thought, looking at her approvingly. She was pretty as could be, sitting opposite him, mouth pursed in thought, hazel eyes earnestly reflective. The way she wore her shining dark hair added maturity to her appearance, a deliberate effort, he thought, to live up to her job. At this moment, though, she looked more like a little girl masquerading as a successful businesswoman. Any young man—

he caught himself up in mid-thought with an inward grin. Who was he trying to kid with his fatherly attitude? He wasn't that old himself.

Gibb Blaine was one of the names Lucia gave him. "His name's really Gilbert," she explained. "His father's at the bank."

"I know. I met him. But the son's not listed as working there."

"No. He's an engineer and he's with a construction firm in Seattle now."

The postal inspector rummaged in his memory. "Seattle? Wasn't he rather serious about you? You mentioned something—"

"Yes. But I was never serious about him."

"Oh." Madden studied her, her open expression, candid gaze, and decided to take her into his confidence a little, dismissing Gibb Blaine for the moment. He said, "Mr. Blaine, as well as Miss Ross, got one of the letters. They're accused of having an affair."

Lucia started, laughed protestingly. "That's the most ridiculous thing I ever heard of," she declared. "Miss Ross is a prim old maid and Mr. Blaine's a mouse. Nice, but still a mouse who spends his life under Mrs. Blaine's thumb. A conventional mouse too. I'm sure he'd never dream of having an affair with another woman, even if he thought he could get away with it."

Her vehemence drew a smile from Madden. "You make his wife sound quite the tyrant."

"She is. Not the obvious kind, though. She's oh so sweet and charming when you meet her, so absorbed in good works. Lots of people think she's wonderful. But according to things Gibb said and things I noticed myself when I was going out with him she always gets her own way. Her heart acts up or she has nervous spells or something if she doesn't."

"How did Gibb Blaine take it when he didn't get his

own way?" Madden inquired. "Did he have a nervous spell over your turning him down?"

Lucia laughed. "No indeed. I didn't ever encourage him, he knew all along that I wasn't seriously interested, but I guess he thought he'd just try his luck anyway. He's certainly not writing the letters. He's in Seattle, no mistake about it. His father brought in a letter from him just the other day."

"You parted friends then?"

"Of course we did. Gibb's heart was far from being broken. He's not the type for it. He's too fond of Gibb for anything like that. His people—his mother, at least—did her part in making him self-centered."

"Parents," Madden commented, "get all the blame these days."

"They should," Lucia asserted uncompromisingly. "I'm darned good and sure I'm not going to spoil my children. They're going to learn to stand on their own feet."

Gibb Blaine, Madden gathered, hadn't learned that. He'd stood on his parents'. He couldn't, though, be writing the letters from Seattle and having them mailed by someone in Fairmount; not with all the short-range information they contained on Lucia.

Madden's thoughts turned to Mr. and Mrs. Blaine. They were right on the scene. How had they reacted to Lucia's rejection of their son?

Lucia, asked about this, said that there had been no particular reaction from them. She didn't see much of Mrs. Blaine, but whenever she did see her, the older woman was as gracious as ever. "Relieved probably," Lucia added, "that I didn't snag her son. She wouldn't think any girl was good enough for him."

As for Mr. Blaine, she continued, his manner toward her at the bank was unchanged. "It would be, anyway, no matter how he felt inside," she said. "He doesn't like arguments."

Keep the peace at any price, Madden reflected. Keeping the peace wouldn't allow room for writing poison pen letters. . . .

A moment later Lucia remarked pensively, "You have to suspect just about everybody in a case like this, don't you? And find out all you can about them?"

"That's right."

"You know," she went on, "until this started and I met you and Rod, I never gave a thought to the post office. But now I'm beginning to realize there's much more to it than just delivering mail and sending it out."

"Indeed there is."

"For one thing, they get to know quite a lot about what goes on, don't they?"

"Sooner or later," Madden informed her, "almost every bit of gossip there is in a town finds its way to the local post office. People talk, you see. How they do talk. To clerks on the windows, to letter carriers on their routes. And people's mail in itself is quite revealing, too. Suppose, for instance, you subscribe to some subversive publication. Your letter carrier, the distributors sorting the mail, could tell me about it."

"Would they even know who I correspond with?"

"To some extent and over a period of time, yes. Out-of-state postmarks that turned up regularly in your mail and so forth."

"What else would they know about me?"

Madden was amused by Lucia's questions. She was, it seemed, identifying herself with Rod, taking an interest in his work. He said, "Oh, the bills you receive, social security checks, dividend checks, correspondence with brokerage firms, bank statements—all that would tell them something about your financial position."

She laughed. "The answer is not to get any mail if you want complete privacy in your life."

"In an investigation that would raise questions too," Madden pointed out. "If the post office tells me someone gets nothing but junk mail, I want to know why. I want to know if that person is just alone and friendless or if there's another reason, such as living under an assumed name."

He came to a halt and then added, "Post office workers don't have to be particularly curious or prying to get all this, you understand. Handling the mails day after day, they're bound to notice things. Sometimes it adds up to quite a lot when I'm looking for information on someone."

"I suppose it does," Lucia said. "It's really fascinating when you stop to think about it."

"But it's not doing much for me at the moment," Madden reminded her lightly.

A few minutes later he left and, although it was getting on toward eight o'clock when he reached Dunston, he stopped at his office before going home to fix himself a belated dinner. He now had twenty-five K documents, counting the one from Mrs. Cummings' typewriter, already mailed. Sorting out the rest, collected at the bank today, and putting aside those that were totally dissimilar, sixteen K documents remained. He also had another Q document, the letter Lucia had turned over to him tonight. He numbered it Q-10 and before he put it in the big manila envelope with the other documents he read it again with the same uneasiness he'd felt when he first read it. He wrote *Please Expedite* and sent it air mail to Washington.

Chapter Nine

The next morning the postal inspector lost no time in giving his aide the new list of names Lucia had supplied and told him to get started on it right away. This was Friday.

Monday morning before he'd finished going through his mail he had a call from Mr. Hasbrouck informing him that he'd received another letter Saturday, sent to his home address, and that Mr. Jenner had also received one. "Mine's a carbon copy of his," Mr. Hasbrouck continued. "It has quite a lot to say about several people who work here. Can you come out this morning, Inspector? Mr. Jenner and I would like to talk to you about it."

"I'll be right out," Madden told him.

"Oh, good. I'll get in touch with Mr. Jenner and let him know you're on your way."

When Madden arrived at the bank he found Mr. Jenner seated beside Mr. Hasbrouck's desk, and after one appraising glance decided that he was a formidable character.

As soon as they were introduced and Madden offered a chair, the board chairman said truculently, "We've never had anything like this before, Inspector, not since the bank was founded back in 1921. I was one of the

91

founders. I know."

His glance was as severe as if Madden himself were to blame for the letters; and when he said founders, it had the sound of something sacred, like Founding Fathers of the Republic.

"It's got to be stopped at once," he said next. "We can't have it."

Mr. Hasbrouck intervened. "Inspector Madden has assured me he's doing his best to clear it up, Claude."

The board chairman's expression served for an answer. It said that Madden's best was far from being good enough.

"May I see the letters?" the latter inquired.

Mr. Hasbrouck handed them across the desk.

They were identical, one a carbon of the other, the salutations typed in separately. The paper was the same Concord bond, the envelopes of the same dime-store quality that had been used all along. The postmark on both was 7 P.M., February 14, the previous Friday. Home addresses having been used, they hadn't come under the cover the post office had put on the bank's mail.

Like the others, they were well constructed and well typed; somewhat profane but not obscene. None of those sent to the bank officials had been obscene. Deference to the status of the recipients? Madden wondered. If so, wasn't it the natural deference of someone working at the bank to a superior?

He read the original first. It said:

Dear Mr. Jenner:

Isn't it time you came down off that goddam throne of yours and caught on to the kind of people you have working for you in your piddling little bank?

God, how you make me sick! And God, how some of the people in that bank make me sick! I don't know which is worse, you going around like Christ walking on the waters or the airs they put on with their pipsqueak jobs.

Let's remove the rose-colored glasses and take a good look at some of them. Like Ben Davidson who hopes he's going to be made a vice-president in spite of having a police court record. Did he ever tell you about that? I guess not! Well, ask him about it, ask him about the jam he got into in July, 1934. It's right on record in Newton, Pa. The charge against him and another man was indecent assault, which in his case meant homosexualism. Nowadays Ben Davidson is a real he-man type but he wasn't back then, ha, ha! Ask him about it. Or ask that snobbish wife of his. But maybe she doesn't know about it herself.

Charges of alley cat morals against Lucia, of adultery against Alec Blaine and Lila Ross were repeated next in the letter. Then a new name, Fred Bauer, appeared.

"If," the letter said, "he's such a responsible employee, the treasurer of the bank, why doesn't he take better care of his daughter Frieda? Why doesn't he keep her home nights? Fifteen's young to be running the streets until all hours, picking up boys and sneaking them into the house when her father's out at some meeting trying to prove what a big shot he is. Ask him how he's going to find a father for Frieda's baby when she ends up pregnant. With all the boys that hang around her she won't be able to name the right one herself."

There were two more names in the letter. Calvin Eads, teller, was accused of alcoholism, of being so hung over when he went to work in the morning that he couldn't speak a civil word to the bank's customers. And where the letter asked, did he get the money to drink so much? Maybe the bank examiners would be able to answer that

93

question sometime.

Elliot Bentham, assistant cashier, the last person named, was accused of being the father of a child born out of wedlock to Mrs. Farmer, a widow who ran a local restaurant.

When Madden had read it he glanced through the carbon to see if any changes had been made. There were none. It was addressed to Mr. Hasbrouck and was an exact duplicate of Mr. Jenner's original.

He looked up to find the board chairman staring at him fixedly out of sharp blue eyes. "Pretty thing, isn't it?" he snapped. "A real pretty thing to come in your morning's mail."

"Vicious. Slanderous," Madden replied in his quietest voice. "May I keep these? I'd like to have them initialed and dated and send them along for examination."

"You can have them and welcome," Mr. Jenner stated. "I've made notes of the charges."

His tone was so grim that Madden felt moved to remind him, "Anonymous ones, Mr. Jenner."

"I realize that. But they'll have to be investigated. Some of them, of course, aren't open to proof. We'll look into them, though. The bank comes first, and if any of this gets out it will do us no good." Claude Jenner's lined old face was as grim as his tone as he continued, "Davidson, for instance. In his case, the charge can be easily proved or disproved. Mr. Hasbrouck and I were talking about it before you came, Inspector. He's in line for promotion, but first there's this thing. Indecent assault. Homosexualism." He wrinkled his nose as if the very words had a horrid smell. "We've located Newton on the map. It's near Pittsburgh, and Mr. Hasbrouck will take a plane out there tomorrow and see what he can find out. Homosexualism. Of all things."

"Perhaps Mr. Davidson himself—?" Madden began, and was interrupted by the little old board chairman who

94

said, "Oh yes, Mr. Hasbrouck will have a talk with him before tomorrow. I hope that meets with your approval, Inspector."

Madden's dislike of him gained ground by the minute, but his voice betrayed none of this feeling as he said, "I'd like to talk with him myself. Whether or not the charge is true, I want to find out from him or who in Fairmount might have heard about it through someone in Newton."

"Oh, I see what you mean." For the first time Mr. Jenner looked on Madden with something approaching favor. "It's not the kind of thing every Tom, Dick, and Harry would know."

Mr. Hasbrouck remarked glumly, "I must say I don't look forward to talking to Davidson about it." He eyed the inspector with hope dawning on his face. "But you'll want to see him first, I guess. Awkward to bring up."

"Awkward? The whole thing's disgraceful, that's what it is." Now it was Mr. Hasbrouck at whom the little old board chairman was looking accusingly, a look that said it was one of his duties to prevent such occurrences at the bank. He continued, "As for Miss Ruyter, I know how you feel, Dick, but I don't go along with it. She's at the heart of it, if it wasn't for her I doubt that it would ever have started. We've got to let her go, accept her resignation as of today. Then we'll see what happens. Dollars to doughnuts, the whole thing will stop dead, there won't be another letter."

"Well, we don't know for sure about that, Claude. And it's most unfair to Miss Ruyter—" Mr. Hasbrouck's voice dragged with doubt and indecision.

Madden went to Lucia's aid. He said to the board chairman, "I can't say I share your feeling that the letters will stop if you let Miss Ruyter go. It's been my experience, Mr. Jenner, that once they start in most poison pen writers seem to develop a compulsion to keep it up. Destructive instinct or something. Getting rid of

Miss Ruyter won't necessarily appease it."

Mr. Jenner glowered at him. "We're not exactly getting rid of her the way you make it sound, Inspector. She handed in her resignation of her own accord. All that remains is to act on it."

"Well . . ." Madden let it rest there, but his tone was eloquent of his opinion of this sort of quibble.

Mr. Jenner, although still glowering, seemed ready, too, for the moment, to let it rest there.

Mr. Hasbrouck sent Madden a glance of gratitude. The latter reflected that Lucia must have more than proved her worth to the bank president for him to stand up to Jenner as much as he had to keep her job for her.

It was the postal inspector who broke the short silence. "If you have a room where I can talk in privacy to these people, Mr. Hasbrouck, I'd like to get started. Davidson first, and then I'll see the others."

"Certainly. You can use the board of directors' room."

Claude Jenner's face revealed his discontent even before he remarked, "The minute you start seeing them it's going to be all over the bank."

Madden looked at him. "It's probably all over the bank already, Mr. Jenner."

"Yes, it probably is. And by tomorrow it will be the talk of Fairmount."

The board chairman was going to be a nuisance, Madden told himself, while he replied patiently, "I really don't know of a way to conduct an investigation without asking questions of the people involved."

"That's right, Claude," Mr. Hasbrouck said. "It can't be helped."

Madden rose. "If you'll show me where the room is, and send for Mr. Davidson, I'll get started."

The board chairman started to speak, thought better of it, stood up, and reached for his hat and coat. Madden said good-by to him.

"I'll be seeing you again, no doubt," Mr. Jenner told him sourly. "I hope you're going to show us some fast results in getting the case cleared up, that's all." He nodded to the bank president. "Call me later, Dick. Let me know how things are going."

"Yes, I'll do that." Mr. Hasbrouck looked relieved when he left and said to Madden in a tone faintly apologetic, "Wonderful old fellow for his age, Inspector. Nothing gets by him, his mind's still sharp as a razor. But, of course, he grew up in a different age when things were done differently. In his day men like him cracked the whip and everyone jumped. He can't seem to realize how much times have changed."

He didn't want to realize it, the inspector thought. His reason for being, his chief occupation was to bedevil the bank president and everyone else in the bank.

Madden hoped that if Mrs. Jenner was still alive she cracked the whip over her husband at home.

Ben Davidson, as tall as Madden, older, into his forties, with strong handsome features and the carriage of an athlete, came into the room assigned to Madden with the ease of a man content with himself and his world. This and the friendly interest with which he greeted the postal inspector vanished instantly when the latter told him why he was there and then read aloud what the letter said about him.

He seemed devastated. He could say nothing at first, just looking at Madden, swallowing again and again as if his mouth had gone completely dry. At last he was able to speak. "My God," he said. "That thing—so long ago—no one around here ever knew about it—dragged up after all these—" His voice cracked, the stricken gaze he fastened on the postal inspector pleaded to be told that it was all a mistake.

Madden said, "Someone in Fairmount knows about it, Mr. Davidson. There have been several of these letters.

They all have a Fairmount postmark and are being written by someone working in the bank or otherwise connected with it."

The older man was beginning to rally from the blow he had received. "I don't see how anyone could have found out. The only person I've ever told the story to is my wife, and that was years ago before we were married. And, I can assure you, Inspector, she'd never repeat it to anyone or write such letters as you're talking about. I don't see how—" He broke off, trying to assemble his thoughts.

What he said about his wife's innocence in the matter the inspector neither believed nor disbelieved. Mrs. Davidson knew what had happened to her husband in Newton, Pennsylvania. That was the important point in what he had just told Madden (who) had long ago discovered, that women were sometimes astonishingly indiscreet in the bits of personal history they revealed to each other. Mrs. Davidson, for example, confiding in her best friend, might have told the whole story.

When Madden voiced this possibility her husband shook his head emphatically. "Never!" he declared. "Hetty has too much sense to trust anyone with a story like that. Why should she bring it up, anyway? It's not a subject we discuss every day, in fact we never talk about it, it's virtually forgotten. I felt she had a right to know about it before she married me, we talked it over then and that was the end of it. I don't believe it's ever been mentioned by either of us the whole eighteen years we've been married. There was no reason it should be. It was a nasty little business, but it turned out all right and was no longer important."

His voice took on a heavier note. "Not until now, that is. But now, Jenner, Hasbrouck—" He eyed Madden in despair. "How stinking mean can people get? How could anyone spread a thing like that around, especially when, knowing the story, they know I was the victim, that I—"

He stopped short and then said, "I guess I'd better tell you the whole thing, Inspector, and let you judge for yourself."

"Cigarette?" Madden suggested and brought them out. Ben Davidson took one, bent his handsome graying head to the light the inspector offered, and began in a precise, even tone, "The summer of 1934 I took a job as a counselor at a boys' camp outside Newton. That was my second summer there. I'd finished my freshman year at college and passed my eighteenth birthday six months before. I came from a small town in Ohio, I went to a small college, and I was green as grass. . . ."

He went on with the shabby little story of an older man in charge of arts and crafts making friends with him, the hours off duty that they spent together, the trips to Newton in the older man's car to see a movie or drop in at a tavern for a few glasses of beer, Ben Davidson feeling adventurous over this, his first drinking, and over not being challenged on his age, easily passing for twenty-one since he had attained his full growth and was as tall then as he was now. All of it, he said, led up to the night when, after more beer than they usually had, the older man made advances in the car outside the tavern. This brought on a fight, the arrival of the police, their arrest with the camp director frantically pulling strings to keep the whole affair quiet, but not able to keep it from becoming a permanent part of the police files in Newton.

"I was green as grass," Ben Davidson repeated at the end. "If I hadn't been, I'd have caught on to what he was long before that night and kept away from him."

Madden, knowing the story, so easily subject to proof, must be true, remarked, "Well, I guess most of us are green as grass at eighteen, Mr. Davidson. What happened to you has happened to plenty of other kids that age."

"You're right, Inspector." Ben Davidson smiled wryly. "But not many of them, I hope, get hit over the head with it like this nearly twenty-five years later."

He had nothing more to tell Madden. He insisted he had never mentioned the affair to anyone in Fairmount or elsewhere; and he was equally insistent that his wife hadn't mentioned it. Why should they, he said; it certainly wasn't anything to be proud of. He knew no one who had moved to Fairmount from Newton, no one who had ever spoken of having friends or relatives there. Someone who had attended the summer camp where he had worked? It had closed up twenty years ago, he had lost all track of the people he had known there. He had received none of the poison pen letters himself and hadn't known until he heard it from Madden that others at the bank were receiving them. If he or his wife should receive one, they would turn it over to Madden immediately, he said, and the interview was over.

After lunch the postal inspector saw the other men mentioned in the letter to the bank officials. He saw Fred Bauer first, a cold man, who grew colder still on hearing what the letter said about his teen-age daughter, with something changing in his eyes that made Madden wonder if this man wasn't a harsh father who had forgotten the follies of his own youth—if he had ever been human enough to indulge in any—and would show little understanding of his daughter's.

He had no information to give the postal inspector. He had received no letters, and stated flatly that they must be the work of a crank. He had no enemies who would include his name or his daughter's in one of them.

He had no friends either, Madden suspected.

At the end of the interview Fred Bauer suggested that in his view all such letters should be destroyed as soon as they were received. No one should attach enough importance to them to call in the postal authorities.

He spoke in a measured voice. But the look that made Madden uneasy remained in his eyes, boding ill for the daughter at home, indicating that he wouldn't take his own advice.

The looseness, the soft used look of self-indulgence advertised itself on the face of Calvin Eads, teller, accused of alcoholism, an accusation, Madden felt, that wasn't yet quite true, with heavy daily drinking being nearer the mark.

His manner was domineering, trying to assert that he was as good as or better than anyone else he met. But he laughed too loud and too scornfully in denial of what the letter said about him, and his burned-out eyes never once met Madden's. He'd heard there were letters going the rounds, he said. Who had told him? He didn't remember.

No, he hadn't received any of them himself and neither had his wife. No, he had no children. "None that I claim anyway," he added with a knowing grin. Trouble with people who came to his station? Nothing of consequence. Most people were, of course, so goddam dumb that they couldn't make out a deposit slip and get it right, and there were other difficulties, minor ones, now and then, such as any teller would expect to have with the bank's customers. But nothing major had occurred, nothing that might have led someone to write a pack of lies about him to the president and the board chairman.

He had second thoughts on this. Some people were jealous of anybody with a good job. His job gained stature in pointing this out to Madden. Neighbors—he named two or three he'd had arguments with—hell, you didn't know what they'd do.

He rambled on into third thoughts. A frustrated old maid might be writing the letters. Menopause made them do funny things. You never could tell.

Madden got rid of Calvin Eads as fast as he could and watched him, fat and sluggish, take his time in leaving the room. If you hit him he'd squash, Madden thought with a grimace.

Elliot Bentham, assistant cashier, a meager facsimile of a man, turned white with horror over the charge that he was the father of the widowed Mrs. Farmer's illegitimate child. Or perhaps it wasn't the charge, Madden reflected, assessing the desiccated appearance of the assistant cashier; perhaps the mere thought of such robust activity was enough to rob him of color.

He almost lost his voice in his breathless haste to lodge a protest. Why, he didn't even know Mrs. Farmer, he declared, and had never eaten so much as one meal in her restaurant. He never ate in restaurants, never poisoned his system with the food they served. He had his own little apartment, bought his own food, did all his own cooking. No fats, no meat. Never meat. Pure poison.

That was the key to the man's whole make-up, Madden told himself. No meat.

Health foods were the thing, Elliot Bentham continued. Goat's milk, goat cheese, wheat germ, raw vegetables. If people would only stick to the right food, they'd never know what a sick day was.

The inspector listened with polite attention while he rode his hobby, and after a decent interval eased him out of the room.

Bentham's name, he thought, had been included in the letter as a malicious joke; and if he knew Mrs. Farmer the joke might take on even more point with her turning out to be a gusty type of woman with earth-bound appetites.

From the bank Madden went to see Mrs. Davidson, and soon after he met her was certain that she hadn't written the letters and would never have told anyone the story of her husband's arrest.

The Davidson house was big and sprawling without pretense of style. In the back yard several small boys were shooting a basketball through a hoop fastened to a post, and in the front yard the postal inspector had to pick his way through a tangle of bicycles to reach the front door. His ring was answered by a tall boy of sixteen or so who admitted him, turned toward the rear of the house, yelled, "Ma, someone to see you," and went back to his gang collected in a room off the hall.

A door at the far end of the hall opened and Mrs. Davidson appeared, eying Madden with an air of reserve, a firming of the mouth that told him she thought he was a salesman and didn't intend to buy a thing.

About forty, she looked a little heavy in a sweater and skirt, her black hair showed streaks of gray, her face was intelligent and pleasant rather than pretty.

When Madden introduced himself her eyes revealed no more than puzzlement. Her husband, apparently, hadn't called her but was waiting until he got home to tell her what had happened at the bank that day.

Mrs. Davidson glanced into the room where her older son's gang was congregated and then took the inspector into a room opposite it, a den where books were scattered around, a typewriter stood on a desk, and on a window seat a teen-aged girl in a sweater and jeans was stretched out flat doing her homework with music blaring from a radio on a table beside her.

"Jeanie." Mrs. Davidson raised her voice to make herself heard. "Turn off the radio and take your homework up to your room, please."

"Okay." Jeanie turned off the radio, looked at the inspector, looked again when she saw how good looking he was, and scrambled to her feet.

"My daughter Jean . . . Mr. Madden."

He nodded and smiled at the girl, and then his glance strayed to the typewriter, noting that it was a Royal standard, that no paper or envelopes were in sight on the desk.

Jeanie left the room, closing the door at her mother's direction, taking a last look at Madden as she did so.

Mrs. Davidson invited him to sit down and sat down

herself. With the closed door muting the sounds of activity from across the hall, he explained why he was there, not missing her astonishment and distress at what he said, and becoming convinced that this wholesome-looking wife and mother had no more to do with the letters than he had.

But she couldn't suggest who might have written them. Like her husband, she knew of no one in Fairmount who came from Newton or who had any sort of association with the place.

"There is such a person, though, Mrs. Davidson," Madden reminded her. "Everything else is local in origin, but this is something that happened a long time ago and hundreds of miles away. Except through someone in Newton, how could anyone here have found out about it?"

"I don't know," she said helplessly. "I don't know." Then she asked in a low voice, "What did Mr. Jenner and Mr. Hasbrouck say about having someone at the bank with a police record?"

"As the victim in the case, at least your husband's name won't be in the criminal files," he suggested consolingly.

She looked only a little relieved. "But it's still on record. . . . Oh, who would do such a cruel thing to him?"

"I'd hoped you could give me some information on that," Madden replied, and added with a smile, "You know, women talking at bridge parties and so on, a remark being made about somebody's sister-in-law in Newton, something of that sort."

"No," she said. "If I heard it, the very mention of Newton would alert me right away."

"I suppose it would, at that." The inspector's scholarly face reflected his disappointment. Then he asked, "What about Pittsburgh? That's nearby."

104

"I don't remember anything at all being said about places in Pennsylvania. Oh, Philadelphia, yes, but nothing that would be near Newton. I don't see how anyone in Fairmount—"

"Not just anyone," he corrected her. "Someone who works at the bank or has some connection with it."

"A wife, you mean?"

"Perhaps. Do you know many of them?"

They went over names. Mrs. Davidson knew most of the wives but none was a close friend. She said, "Oh no," disconcertedly when Madden told her that she was described as snobbish in the letter."

"I'm not," she said next. "Really I'm not."

He inquired into her background. It was a substantial one. She'd always lived in Fairmount, her father, in his lifetime, had been on the board of directors of the bank, she'd met her husband after he started working there in 1937. A college classmate, son of the then president, had gotten him the job. But the classmate had been killed in the war, his father had died ten years ago, the classmate hadn't even known about the Newton affair anyway, it was a dead end.

Mrs. Davidson had never, she insisted, snubbed anyone at the bank or done anything to their families that would justify calling her snobbish. She kept coming back to that point. It disturbed her.

But Madden, reading between the lines, told himself that there were sins of omission as well as commission. Mrs. Davidson, her own social position secure, chose her friends as she pleased, and in the exercise of this right could have inadvertently hurt more than one person's feelings.

A woman would be quicker than a man to notice and resent that sort of selectivity, he told himself next. And wasn't snobbish a woman's choice of word?

Mrs. Davidson followed him out to the porch when he

left. "My poor husband," she said. "I'm so worried about him. He must be terribly upset."

The inspector offered what reassurance he could, but the worried look remained on her face until her younger son came bounding up the steps clamoring for apples for himself and his friends. She summoned a smile for him, and that was the image Madden carried away of her, a woman hiding her worry from her child.

He went to the post office. Rod Harrison knew of no one in Fairmount who corresponded with anyone in Newton, Pennsylvania, but he would take it up with the clerks and carriers, he said.

Back in his office in Dunston, Inspector Madden dictated a letter to the Pittsburgh office requesting that a Pittsburgh inspector check the Newton police files on Ben Davidson's arrest and find out from the Newton postmaster if his change of address list for the past two years included one from Newton to the Fairmount area.

Chapter Ten

Inez Blaine took in her mail, two pieces of it, at ten o'clock the next morning. One was a letter from her son Gibb, the other, in what she thought of as an inspired moment, she had written to herself.

She read her son's letter first, his usual weekly letter that said he was fine, everything was fine, he liked his job, but aside from that wasn't doing anything worth writing about at the moment. He expected to fly to San Francisco next week and was looking forward to the trip.

Fly to San Francisco? A furrow appeared between Inez' eyes. Weren't there mountains in that section? A train would be much safer. She'd write and urge him to take a train; tell him it would just worry the life out of her if he persisted in flying.

She opened her own letter and read with objective attention what she had written to herself. It began: "Dear Mrs. Blaine: How long are you going to close your eyes to what's going on between your husband and Lila Ross? She may look like a prim old crow but she wasn't so prim the night she got together with your husband at your house while you were at the VNA board meeting. You ought to have seen what went on!"

The letter, in obscene detail, described the alleged

behavior of Alec and Lila Ross that night. Almost too obscene? Not really, not for the type of person the letters indicated, a lewd, horrible creature worlds removed from her actual self.

Inez finished the letter, put it down, picked it up and read it again. Alec, she thought, and laughed aloud shrilly. Imagine Alec doing the things he was accused of! Alec, who was too timid to even look at another woman.

She felt very much pleased with herself. Her husband, with Dick Hasbrouck to back him up, could prove that what she had written about him wasn't true. She hadn't hurt him at the bank and yet she had him right where she wanted him at home. He thought he'd got away with not telling her about the letter she'd sent to him. She'd make him squirm for that.

Inez went to the phone and called her husband. Her announcement of a letter that said dreadful things about him and Lila Ross bereft him of speech for an interval during which she said over and over, "Dreadful things, Alec. Just dreadful."

But presently, after assuring her repeatedly without hope of being believed that, no matter what the letter said, it wasn't true, Alec, in turn, gave her pause by telling her that Inspector Madden from the post office was investigating several letters that had been sent and that he'd report hers to the inspector right away.

At first she said no, he mustn't do anything of the kind. A moment later she told him to go ahead with it. "Why not?" she thought in a surge of self-confidence. She could hold her own with an inspector from the post office, couldn't she? It might even be interesting to cross swords with him. In fact, she'd run over to the VNA today during the nurses' lunch hour and dash off a letter to Lucia about the entertaining she'd done last night just to show him how little his nosing around meant to her!

Except for Alec Blaine's efforts to soothe his wife, the

day passed quietly at the bank. Mr. Hasbrouck wasn't there. He had left for Pittsburgh on an early morning flight and by noon had hired a car and was on his way to Newton.

Lucia's day was brightened in midafternoon by the arrival of Robert Doucette, a French-Canadian in his early thirties, married, the father of a brood that grew larger year by year, and the owner of a prospering radio and TV repair business. This time, he said as he sat down beside her desk, he had come to take out a chattel mortgage on a new truck.

"New truck?" she commented. "You said when you had your other loan paid off you were going to buy a new car."

"Yeh, yeh. But will a new car they never see impress the customers with how good business is?" He favored her with his exuberant grin. "Besides, you put tree, four kids in a new car they don't do the upholstery no good."

"Th-ree," Lucia corrected him, returning his grin. "Not tree, Mr. Doucette."

They both laughed. His trouble with *th* sounds was a standing joke between them.

She took out an application form and asked for the bill of sale on the truck. He handed it to her and sat back and lit a cigarette while she was filling out the form. "Too bad I can't drive the new truck when I go to Canada next summer," he said. "I guess it don't matter, though. They don't pay much attention to things like that in the village I come from. They're behind the times there. Just think, my brother's wife, she's never even seen a train and they live only twenty miles from a railroad. Did I ever tell you about my brother Armand?"

"I don't think so." Lucia laid down her pen, always ready to listen to Robert Doucette's tales of French Canada.

"Well, he's been married eleven years, and he's got

nine kids and a wife that's never seen a train and gets along fine on his farm."

"Was he in the army too?" Lucia inquired, knowing from past sessions with Robert Doucette that he had been in the States when World War II began and at eighteen had enlisted in the American Army.

He laughed. "Well, not like me, Miss Ruyter. The war wasn't popular in French Canada, you know. We don't like the English. We never have. Father to son we pass on the story of what the English did to our ancestors, driving them off their farms and—"

"Oh, *Evangeline*," Lucia broke in. " 'This is the forest primeval—' "

"*Evangeline*? Yeh, yeh. So we don't like the English, if the Germans lick them, we don't care. We go our way, they can go theirs."

"What about France? Didn't you care when France fell?"

He shrugged. "We don't like France either."

"But you went into our army," she reminded him.

"Because it made it easier for me to become a citizen. But in French Canada they dodged the draft. When MPs from Quebec went out to the villages the young men took to the hills."

"Your brother Armand too?"

"Until the MPs caught him one time when he didn't know they were coming. They took him to Quebec and he put on a big act making out he was crazy. So in a couple of months they let him go."

Lucia laughed. Robert Doucette's recital was too matter-of-fact to leave room for disapproval. He went on, "But then I was taken prisoner a month after D-Day and the first report said I was dead. So Armand got good and mad. For tree—th-ree—days my sister Marie said he didn't do nothing but talk about it. Then he took off for Quebec to enlist. Because now the war, it got personal for him, see?"

110

Lucia said, "I see."

"But in Quebec they didn't want him. They had it on their records from the other time that he was crazy."

"And what did he do about that?" Lucia felt sure that no brother of Robert Doucette's would have been stopped by an adverse psychiatric report once he had made up his mind to enlist in the Canadian Army.

"Well, we have an uncle in Quebec who's in politics. He had influence in lots of places. But it took time and—"

Her phone interrupted the story. It was Rod Harrison. She had another letter, he said, cleared from a downtown box by one of the carriers on his way back to the post office. "I'll drop it off on my way home," he said.

"If you don't mind."

He caught the restraint in her voice. "Someone listening?"

"Yes."

"All right, I'll see you later."

Robert Doucette's shrewd dark eyes were on her as she hung up. She forced a bright smile for him. "You were saying—?"

"Just telling you how my uncle finally got Armand in the army. But the war ended before he got a chance to go overseas. He's always been kind of sorry about that so maybe he wasn't so smart after all."

Lucia's laugh was perfunctory. She had lost interest in life in French Canada, her thoughts were on what her letter would say.

She finished filling out the application form, had Robert Doucette sign it, and within a few minutes she had the chattel mortgage ready for his signature, the check made out, and was saying good-by to him, a satisfied customer of the bank, a favorite customer of hers.

* * *

Inspector Madden received two calls from Fairmount that day, the first from Alec Blaine to tell him about his wife's letter, the second, late in the afternoon, from Rod reporting Lucia's, and the fact that it had been mailed in one of the boxes in the downtown area. But that wasn't much help, he went on to say; several carriers had dumped mail on the face-up table and about fifteen boxes were involved. "All we know for sure is that it wasn't mailed in an outlying neighborhood," Rod concluded.

Madden said, "Blaine's wife got one today. I'm going to see them tonight."

"We missed that one," Rod remarked. "We've got a cover on the bank and Lucia's mail and we're keeping an eye out for them generally, but we missed that one."

"Well, don't worry about it. You can't put a cover on all the bank people. They're reporting them themselves, anyway. Now, about Lucia Ruyter's—if you're taking it over to her tonight, I'll stop by and pick it up after I've seen the Blaines."

"All right, I'll tell her to expect you."

After he hung up Madden stayed on at his desk. Consulting his notebook and with a calendar to aid him, he wrote down the date, the day of the week, and the cancellation time for each of the letters brought to his attention so far.

Monday was the most prolific day, eight had been mailed that day. Thursday came next with three, and two each had been mailed on Wednesday and Friday.

Lila Ross had destroyed her letter, Mr. Hasbrouck his first one, so he didn't have the cancellation time on them. The rest, with one exception, had been canceled between 6:30 and 7 P.M., which meant they had been mailed in the late afternoon and picked up in the night collection.

The letter Mrs. Blaine had received today made a total of nine mailed on Monday. Lucia's, mailed today, was the first Tuesday mailing and the second to be mailed in the earlier part of the afternoon.

So far she had been the main target, attacked in the two letters sent to Jenner, the seven to Hasbrouck. Five more, counting today's, had been sent to her. But now the campaign of abuse had begun to broaden out.

There were two possible reasons for this, Madden thought. Other bank people might have been brought into it in a secondary outburst of malice; or they might become collectively the target with Lucia merely leading the list; if the latter were the case, then the motive for the letters wouldn't be found in her private life; it would lie in something that had happened at the bank.

Until he could settle this point he would have to work with both possibilities in mind.

What else did the frequency table tell him?

If the letters were mailed the day they were written—and they weren't the sort of thing anyone would want to carry around very long—then he had a pattern of access to the typewriter every Monday and most Thursdays. The rest of the letters, two each on Wednesday and Friday, today's to Lucia on Tuesday, fell into no particular pattern. None at all had been written on Saturday or Sunday unless they were carried around until late Monday afternoon before they were mailed.

No week-end access to the typewriter?

Not at the bank certainly. That would be closed over the week end. And if the typewriter was one of the bank's, the paper wasn't theirs. The typing samples he'd collected had told him that.

Madden sighed in irritation. He was all off in his reasoning. How could anyone at the bank be sure of privacy Monday, Thursday, or any other day to sit down at one of the typewriters and write the letters?

It was no use worrying about that right now or about who had the typewriter at home or somewhere else and kept carbon paper on hand to make copies of Jenner's letters for Hasbrouck. Until he had a report from Washington on the Q and K documents he'd sent in, he didn't even know what kind of a typewriter he was looking for.

He should have one soon. He'd sent the first letters to the lab nearly three weeks ago.

Chapter Eleven

That evening Madden paid a visit to the Blaines. They lived in a good neighborhood, their house a two-story colonial, dating back thirty or forty years. A post light turned on at the edge of the driveway, where a pale blue Mercury stood helped him to find the house and another light turned on over the front door guided him up the walk to the steps.

Alec Blaine admitted him. Inez advanced from the living room and smiled and offered her hand, saying, "How do you do, Inspector," in a soft pleasant voice.

Lucia's comments on her came into Madden's mind. Whatever she was like inwardly, on the surface she exuded graciousness and charm, qualities notably lacking in her husband.

She was past fifty, Madden thought, but coping with the years very well, her figure fairly slender and corseted into trimness, her blouse and matching skirt casually expensive looking, hair carefully groomed, make-up not too obvious. Beside her Alec Blaine looked more colorless than ever.

When they were seated in the living room Inez took over, producing her letter, telling him how much it embarrassed her, building up her hesitation over letting him see it.

While Madden reassured her Alec sat upright in a chair, letting her do the talking, go into detail about her feelings when she read the letter, her call to the bank to inform her husband of it.

At last she gave it to Madden, who went through his routine of looking at the envelope and typing, the 7:30 P.M. postmark of the previous day before he took out the letter and read it.

What it said about meetings between Alec Blaine and Miss Ross was mostly very general, he noticed; only one received particular mention, the same one that had been highlighted in the letter sent to Blaine himself.

Before he could comment on it Inez said, "Of course I know what the letter says isn't true, Inspector. I have complete confidence in my husband."

She threw the latter a smile. It bounced off him as if off a wall. No, not a wall, Madden thought, the man wasn't as substantial as that, he was a cipher, reduced to one by Mrs. Blaine. And yet, away from her, he must show some sort of ability. He held a fair job at the bank, not a top job, but one that was fairly good.

"Complete confidence," Inez Blaine repeated firmly, but as she spoke the glance she sent her husband didn't match her words; there was contempt in it, or perhaps it was anger, Madden wasn't sure just how it should be interpreted.

Alec Blaine didn't thank his wife for the faith she expressed in him. His eyes met hers emptily and slid away.

Whether she believed what the letter said or not, Mrs. Blaine was giving him a bad time over it, the inspector thought. But then, wasn't Blaine born to be bullied? Some people were. Nevertheless, he gave the other man what help he could, reminding Inez that the letter revealed little knowledge of her husband's activities, that

116

on the one specific occasion it mentioned he had been at a meeting with Mr. Hasbrouck in Dunston and couldn't have seen Miss Ross.

"Yes, I know," she replied lightly. "Alec brought it up. The writer wasn't so smart that time."

"Not knowing that your husband had a sound alibi?" Madden's tone was as light as hers.

"Yes. Not knowing as much as he otherwise seems to."

"He, Mrs. Blaine? You feel it's a man?"

"Well," she gave a little shudder. "A woman would hardly—"

Madden told her the same thing he had told Lucia about what women were capable of putting into anonymous letters. She arched her brows in polite disbelief, and he dropped the matter.

She said next, "Such a contrast. A letter like that arriving in the same mail with a letter from Gibb—my son. He's working for a construction firm in Seattle. It's a very good job, but I do wish it hadn't taken him so far away."

My son, she said, not our son. Her husband, it seemed, was denied a share in him.

How would a man eventually react to years of that kind of treatment?

Alec Blaine's pallid exterior kept its own counsel.

Inez went on to talk about Gibb, how well he had done in high school and college, how devoted and thoughtful he was, never missing his weekly letter to her.

But he had gotten out from under her thumb, Madden reflected. And Lucia had been unenthused about him.

Madden asked the question he was asking of everyone. "Mrs. Blaine, do you have any idea who could be writing these letters?"

She shook her head. "None, Inspector. I've been thinking about it all day, too, and Alec and I have talked it over. I didn't even know about his or Miss Ross's until

117

mine came, you see. Alec says he didn't mention it because he didn't want to worry me." Her voice held a sharp note as she looked at her husband. "I told him he needn't protect me like that. I'd rather know what's going on than have it take place behind my back."

The inspector felt sorry for Alec Blaine.

Presently she asked what led people to write anonymous letters. Frustration, he told her, a sense of injury, revenge, jealousy were among the most common motives.

"Well!" She turned to her husband with an air of playfulness. "Alec, I'm just a housewife, not mixing with all kinds of people the way you do at the bank. Are you sure it isn't Miss Ross herself writing to you, a secret yearning, perhaps, or the feeling that you've slighted her or something?"

His embarrassment was painful to witness as he said, "Oh no, Inez! Miss Ross has nothing to do with this. She's as much a victim as I am."

Madden came to his aid, inquiring gravely, "Mrs. Blaine, do you really think the letters are being written by Miss Ross?"

"Why, I wasn't serious, Inspector!"

"Well, I wish you would be. It's a serious matter."

"Yes, of course it is," she agreed quickly. "I was just having a little fun with Alec but I suppose I shouldn't." She smiled at Madden, all penitence and charm.

The charm was wasted on him, but his point was made. She wouldn't again, in front of him, taunt her husband over the letters. She would be wary of names now, too, but she had said she had none to give him anyway.

He led the conversation around to how long Alec Blaine had worked at the bank—twenty-nine years—how long they had lived in Fairmount—Alec all his life, Inez since their marriage—how many children they had—just Gibb—and various other personal matters, absorbing information on their backgrounds, some of which he already knew through the personnel files at the bank. Mrs. Blaine came from Dover, Delaware, but that was nowhere near Newton, Pennsylvania. Nothing that they told him seemed pertinent to his case.

He commented on what a nice house they had, and added with complete disregard for the truth that he was thinking of buying one himself. This statement and others equally untruthful had the desired effect. Inez offered to show him around, through the four rooms downstairs, the three rooms up, all furnished with the kind of good taste that was a little too studied, too decorator-inspired for his liking. But upstairs an Underwood portable typewriter innocently in view on a table rewarded his sightseeing tour. Neither of the Blaines referred to it. He had no way of knowing which of them used it or if both of them did.

As soon as the tour was concluded, Madden left, taking Inez Blaine's letter with him.

She smiled in triumph as she closed the door after him.

Rod was at Lucia's ahead of the inspector. The latter met Mrs. Aitken in the vestibule, but she could be dismissed from his mind as soon as he said good evening to her and rang Lucia's bell. Mrs. Aitken had never really figured on his list of suspects.

He felt that his timing was bad, that his ring, bringing Lucia to the door, had interrupted a kiss. She looked self-conscious, and Rod was too busy smoothing back his hair to meet Madden's eye. But by pretending to be blind to their behavior he set them at ease in a moment or two, and Lucia produced her letter.

This one, like its immediate predecessor, carried an implied threat that ran: "You still haven't mended your ways, I see. Don't think I don't know what you were up to last night with your curtains drawn and a man in your apartment until midnight. You're not fooling me with

119

your baby face act. Just keep on the way you're going, but don't say no one ever warned you if the time should come when you're fished out of some river or picked up in some alley. Why don't you quit your dirty ways before it's too late?''

Madden weighed the implied threat, the second one directed at Lucia, in silence. Neither open nor explicit, it only pointed out what might happen to a girl who was promiscuous. Lucia Ruyter wasn't, and would not be placed in the kind of situation mentioned in the letter. It seemed, then, that the intent was merely to frighten her. But beyond that, the fact that someone was keeping a close watch on her couldn't be ignored.

Rod was the first to speak. "I was visiting Lucia last night, Inspector, so I'm the man the letter refers to. She had the curtains drawn because it was a cold night. If they hadn't been, whoever was outside would have known we weren't alone, that I'd brought another couple along, friends of mine, and that we played bridge the whole evening. They came with me in my car, though, and that's why it wasn't known they were here."

"It's not very pleasant to think that I'm being spied on," Lucia remarked to Madden.

"No. But if you mean someone outside your place for hours, I don't think it happened that way. If it had, the other couple would have been seen and there'd have been no point to what the letter says."

"But someone with a mind like that wouldn't care how pointless it was," Lucia said. "They'd still strike out at random, wouldn't they?"

Madden didn't agree. He thought that with one or two exceptions the accusations were far from being random shots, that their viciousness was based on considerable knowledge of the lives of the people to whom they were sent. But it was only to Lucia, their chief victim, that any sort of threat, even an implied one, was made.

This thought brought up again the question of whether

the letters to the others had been all along no more than a subsidiary outlet for envy and malice and hatred.

He said, "I don't think we're dealing with random shots, Miss Ruyter. Too many of them hit the target."

She sighed. "And now I'm being spied on. Last night and probably other nights too. It makes me feel so uncomfortable."

"Of course it does. It's supposed to. But I doubt if it's a regular thing. In the dead of winter anyone outside here on foot or parked in a car would be pretty conspicuous before long. It would be a chance I wouldn't care to take myself."

As he spoke Madden turned off the lights and went to the front windows. The curtains were again drawn. He drew them aside and looked out. The street was deserted with only his and Rod Harrison's cars in sight. Dropping the curtains back in place, he turned on the lights and said to the girl, "It would be safe enough to drive past now and then in the evening but that's certainly not the main source of information on you. Did you mention to anyone today that you'd had company last night? Mrs. Aitken, for instance?"

Lucia shook her head. "Not even to her. She'd know there were people here, of course. She'd hear them. But I haven't talked to her since yesterday afternoon. She's been away all day and just got home when you arrived." After a pause Lucia added with a faint smile and a sidewise glance at Rod, "Anyway, I don't go around saying, 'Guess who I had a date with last night.' I have a little more sense than that, Inspector."

He smiled back at her. "I didn't mean it quite that way. But it could come out casually, you know. You yawned, say, and when that brought a comment from someone that you must be keeping late hours, you might have mentioned playing bridge last night with Rod and his friends."

"I suppose I might have," Lucia conceded, "but I

didn't. If I yawned, no one noticed it. And if bridge was mentioned, it didn't remind me of the hands I played. In other words, Inspector, I said nothing about the evening to anyone. For one thing, I was too busy all day. For another"—a sidewise glance went to Rod seated beside her on the sofa—"I wouldn't have done it even if I hadn't been too busy."

"Well," Madden said, "just to be sure we've covered every angle, do you happen to know what time Mrs. Aitken left for the day?"

"It was very early, about seven-thirty this morning. She went to New York, and I'm sure she didn't have time before she left to gossip about my company last night. She wouldn't anyhow. She's much too nice for that sort of thing."

Madden nodded. Lucia's letter had been mailed before three o'clock this afternoon. Mrs. Aitken, Lucia herself were eliminated as the source of what the letter said.

He asked Rod about the other couple present. They didn't live in Fairmount, Rod said. They'd dropped in on him unexpectedly and he'd brought them along to Lucia's. He himself, he volunteered, hadn't mentioned last night to a soul.

Everyone who might have talked about it was now eliminated, Madden reflected. References to drawn curtains and a man inside could only have come from driving past the house, perhaps more than once, or parking near it sometime during the evening.

A man checking up on the girl? What her last two letters said pointed toward a man, rebuffed in some way that had no meaning for her and great meaning for him. No matter how honest she was in insisting that such a man didn't exist, it needn't be true. Grudges grew to monstrous size at times from the most trifling beginnings. The only trouble with this line of reasoning was that it left out certain expressions in the letters that pointed toward a woman.

Man or woman, pay your money, take your choice, Madden thought, impatient with himself.

He looked at Lucia, the light falling on her smooth dark head as she turned to say something to Rod. She looked very young at that moment, and a little bit like Estelle when he had first met her years ago. There was no actual resemblance between them, it was just a trick of the light. But still, for a moment she had reminded him of Estelle.

He said, "There's one precaution I'd like you to take, Miss Ruyter."

"Precaution?"

"Yes, where men are concerned. I'm having the ones you told me about investigated and so far they all seem to be in the clear, but just the same it would be a good idea for you to give it some thought before you go out with any of them."

"Oh. But none of them work at the bank."

"I know. Still . . . just an extra precaution. Bending over backward, perhaps."

"It seems so to me. However," Lucia spoke resignedly, "I'll go along with it on the grounds that you know best."

"Sure he does," Rod said. "Stick close to the post office, Lucia. Play it safe and don't date anyone except assistant postmasters."

She laughed and glanced at Madden. "How many assistant postmasters have you sent to jail, Inspector?"

He fell in with her mood. "I've lost count there've been so many. Take warning, Miss Ruyter. Very high incidence of nefarious activities among them."

"I'll keep that in mind," she said.

"But seriously—" Madden persisted.

"All right, I'll be very careful. If I should get asked for a date, I'll think long thoughts—"

"Unless it's an assistant postmaster," Rod interjected. "The Fairmount assistant postmaster."

"Okay," she said with mock solemnity.

Madden let it rest there. He didn't want to alarm her, particularly when there might be nothing to become alarmed about. And he had Rod for an ally, he reflected. Rod seemed to be taking up all her evenings and he would look out for her.

Lucia's manner that night deceived both men. When they were gone, Rod an hour later than the inspector, she sat in front of the dying fire and acknowledged to herself that underneath her other feelings toward her unknown enemy ran a current of fear. It was chilling to realize how much she, who had never known hatred before, was hated now; to wonder how long abusive letters would be enough to satisfy that hatred.

She had fitted many faces to her enemy these weeks past. None was right, none suited the role. Sullen or smiling, young or old, plain or handsome, what face did her enemy wear?

Her method had been wrong. Why should she have thought that inner ugliness must sometimes betray itself outwardly? The answer lay elsewhere in character and personality.

She stood up, turned off the lights, and looked out at the dark, silent street. No one in sight. Nearly midnight. No one would be out there at this hour spying on her. She shivered and dropped the curtain.

Before she went to bed she checked her front and back doors to make sure they were locked.

Chapter Twelve

There were no more letters that week, but Friday morning's newspaper carried a report on the fruits of one of them. The headline on the first page FAIRMOUNT HIGH SCHOOL GIRL REPORTED MISSING caught the postal inspector's eye at breakfast. The subhead was: Parents Seek Aid Of Police; the story said that Frieda Bauer, fifteen, had left for school yesterday morning but had failed to return in the afternoon. Her mother, phoning a friend of her daughter's, learned that she hadn't attended school that day. A search of her room revealed a note in which the high school sophomore stated that she was leaving home for good. Her father, treasurer of the Fairmount Bank and Trust Company, had reportedly informed police that the night before his daughter's disappearance she had expressed resentment over certain restrictions he had laid down governing her activities outside of school hours and that he believed this might have led her to running away. The story concluded with a description of the girl and the clothes she was wearing at the time of her disappearance.

At his usual breakfast spot Madden laid aside his paper and devoted himself to the bacon and eggs the waitress set before him. But his thoughts were on what he had just read and the replies he made to her friendly remarks were absent-minded.

He pictured cold-eyed Fred Bauer lashing out at his daughter over what was said about her in the letter; and the girl, whether it was true or not, defending herself, denying everything.

There must have been some harsh scenes at the Bauers', given a man like the father. What part had Mrs. Bauer played in them? The mediator, trying to placate both husband and daughter; the Mrs. Fred Bauers often were, their husbands saw to that.

Madden's thoughts went to Inez Blaine and her husband the downtrodden figure in their marriage. What would she be like, married to Bauer? That wouldn't happen, though. People tended to marry someone whose personality supplemented theirs, filled some need or supplied some contrast. Male bullies didn't marry female bullies. Each sought someone to dominate. . . .

The inspector ate his breakfast, went to his office, and there found in the morning mail the report he had been waiting for from Washington.

It stated that exhibits Q-1 to Q-8 and K-1 to K-17 had been examined, and the findings were as follows: Exhibits Q-1 to Q-8 had been written on the same typewriter, the type that of a Smith Corona portable, manufactured prior to 1950. The style name was Pica. The manufacturer could not be further identified, since one manufacturer's type could be readily substituted on another manufacturer's machine. The crossbar of the capital *T* and the tail of the comma were badly worn. These and other peculiarities did not appear on exhibits K-1 to K-17, none of which had been typed on the same machine as exhibits Q-1 to Q-8. Such fingerprints as were developed on exhibits Q-1 to Q-8 were fragmentary impressions unsuitable for comparison purposes.

The envelopes included in exhibits Q-1 to Q-8, the

eport continued, were of a quality that could be found in ive-and-ten-cent stores and other similar outlets. The aper used in writing exhibits Q-1 to Q-8 contained the watermark *Old Concord Bond* and was made of 25 per cent cotton fiber. The paper was sold to printers on a non-control basis, and the specific date of its manufacture could not be determined since it did not bear a date code.

A list of seven dealers in the Dunston area who sold Old Concord Bond came next. The report then went on to state that, examined under oblique light, no ghost writing or other impressions had been brought out on exhibits Q-1 to Q-8. No hairs, lipstick, or other foreign substance had been found adhering to the flaps of the envelopes. An additional report would follow on exhibits Q-9 to Q-13, submitted since the previous findings were completed.

Madden put the report away in the file he was building up on E 12133, the number assigned to the case. He was no longer working in the dark on the typewriter, he had a particular machine to look for now, a Smith Corona portable manufactured prior to 1950.

The paper offered less hope. Tracing the sale of it, if it had been a cash transaction, would be virtually impossible. If it had been charged, it had probably been bought from one of the dealers in the Dunston area, and there was a chance that their files on charge customers might turn up a lead for him. But the typewriter, he thought, promised more. He would try it first.

He called in his investigative aide and asked him to start checking typewriter agencies in Dunston—there was none, he knew, in Fairmount—for sales of second-hand Smith Corona portables in the past few months.

A little later, the rest of his mail and other desk matters attended to, Madden left for Fairmount and went first to the bank. As soon as he stepped inside he caught the atmosphere of subdued excitement, caused by Frieda Bauer's disappearance, that pervaded it. The girl's father he reflected, would have his supporters, his detractors, and there would be others who would simply deplore what had happened and feel sorry for the whole family. Whatever their individual feelings, by nightfall they would have spread the story far and wide and everyone in Fairmount who hadn't yet heard about the poison pen letters would hear about them now and that Frieda Bauer's disappearance was tied in with them. Any hopes the bank officials might have had of keeping the affair to some extent quiet were torn to shreds.

Mr. Hasbrouck confirmed this thought when Madden was seated in his office. "Terrible thing about the Bauer girl," he began, shaking his bald head. "Terrible. I feel sorry for Fred and his wife and for the girl too. Fred's not in today, of course, but I talked to him on the phone. He's all upset, naturally. It's that letter, Inspector, what it said about his daughter. Fred took it up with her as any father would. But too bad, too bad." Mr. Hasbrouck sighed heavily. "Mr. Jenner was just on the phone to me. He's in quite a state. I said to him, 'Claude, we might as well face it. There's not a hope now of keeping any part of this thing under cover. Not a hope. The Bauer girl's disappearance has finished that for good.' That's what I said to him. But he's still insisting I'm to tell people here that they're not to say a thing about it outside. I guess I told you, Inspector, that he lives in a different world. He can't be made to see that it's out of the question to tell people it's as much as their job is worth to mention this outside the bank. Claude thinks you can. Makes things difficult. Very difficult."

Mr. Hasbrouck came to a full stop, took out a handkerchief, and wiped his forehead and the top of his head. "Inspector, do you know yet who's writing the letters?" It was a plea for help.

"No, not yet. But I know what kind of a typewriter they're written on and that's what I want to talk to you

128

about, Mr. Hasbrouck."

"Oh. Well, I'll be only too—" The older man broke off as his telephone rang and visibly braced himself to pick up the receiver. He said, "Hello?" and then, "Oh, it's you, Claude. . . . Did you? . . . No, you couldn't get him at his office because he isn't there—I mean, well, he's here. . . . No, Claude, no, he hasn't. . . ."

The wire buzzed and crackled. Mr. Hasbrouck, looking acutely unhappy, said at intervals, "Yes, Claude," and "Yes, I know," and "Yes, I'm sure he is, Claude," from which Madden inferred that he himself was being denounced for not having already served up the letter writer's head on a platter.

"The typewriter," Mr. Hasbrouck managed to get in at last. "He knows what kind is being used so he's that much more ahead, Claude."

Unappeased, the wire crackled some more. Finally Mr. Hasbrouck said, "All right, Claude. Yes, I'll call you right away. I'll keep in close touch with you all day. . . . Yes, Claude."

He hung up and regarded Madden with utter dejection, until he became aware of what his expression must be and replaced it with a feeble smile. "Mr. Jenner's upset," he explained superfluously.

"Yes, I suppose he is."

"So am I," Mr. Hasbrouck added and then, in a burst of petulance, "I must confess I don't understand the way teen-agers act today. People don't seem to be able to handle their children any more. They run wild, do as they please. . . ." His voice died away, picked up as he continued, "I can't get over that girl running away from a good home. You never used to hear of things like that."

The postal inspector kept his thoughts on the Bauer home to himself.

Mr. Hasbrouck said next, "Oh, the typewriter. What about it, Inspector?"

"I've had a report from Washington. It's a Smith Corona portable with pica type."

"We don't have a portable in the bank," the older man asserted instantly.

"I know. The report is negative on the samples you gave me."

"Well, that's good." Mr. Hasbrouck's relieved sigh was short-lived as Madden went on to say that he'd like to have a check made of typewriters bank employees had at home and have each person who owned one bring in a two-page, single-spaced sample with the make, model, and owner's name included.

"But—" The bank president looked perplexed. "If it's someone here, they'd know the minute they were asked that it would be a dead giveaway to bring in a sample."

Madden smiled. "Yes, but after I get all I can I'll do a follow-up if it seems necessary. Check and double-check for switches or omissions. Also," he went on, "I'd like to have the employees urged to produce any letters they've received that we don't know about. Stress the fact that they can be put in sealed envelopes to be turned over to me so nobody needs to get embarrassed about it."

Mr. Hasbrouck said yes to whatever he suggested. At this point, Madden recognized, he would have agreed to produce a sample from a Martian's typewriter if asked for one.

Presently he spoke of his trip to Newton. The police had been very helpful, he said, bringing out everything they had in their files on Ben Davidson's arrest.

"I was glad to learn," he continued, "that it happened just as Ben said. I talked it over with Mr. Jenner as soon as I got back and told him the whole story. He was just as pleased as I was about it."

Madden, who found it hard to believe that Claude Jenner was ever pleased about anything, remarked, "Well then, your trip was worth while, Mr. Hasbrouck.

Davidson's cleared and still in line for his promotion."

"Promotion? Oh yes." A shade of reserve crept into the older man's voice. "We haven't discussed that yet, Mr. Jenner and I."

Madden said nothing more. In spite of being cleared, Ben Davidson's standing had been permanently impaired in Mr. Jenner's eyes.

From the bank the inspector went to the post office. Rod had already taken his break for lunch, but he accompanied the inspector to a restaurant and had coffee with him while he ate.

Madden ordered, and when the waitress went away they talked a little about Frieda Bauer. Then Madden told Rod about the report on the typewriter, and Rod said he would keep his eyes and ears open to see if he could find out anything about it.

A moment later Madden inquired, "How many collection boxes are there in Fairmount, Rod?"

"Thirty-two."

"Well, I'm going to have to ask you to keep the night collection from each box separate."

"Oh lord, the heaviest collection of the day. What a job that's going to be."

"I know. But look at the pattern. All but two of the letters have turned up in the night collection."

"Okay." Rod's tone was resigned. He added, "Be a hell of a lot easier if they were mailed first thing in the morning. The typewritten addresses would really stand out among all the handwritten stuff, the letters to Aunt Mamie, the checks to the light and telephone companies, and so on. But things never do work out the easy way."

"No, they don't."

"Well, I'll set it up as of tonight. How long do you suppose we'll need to keep it going?"

"Let's try it for a week and see what happens."

The younger man nodded. It wasn't necessary for

Madden to voice the thought that something probably would, now that a mailing time had been established. Rod, as well as he, knew that the writer wasn't apt to mail the letters all over town using in turn each of the thirty-two collection boxes. People fell into the habit of using certain ones; the one nearest home, a particular box in the downtown area. The writer might be clever enough to avoid the box nearest home; but if a different one was used, it was likely to be on the route followed in going to work or in some other convenient spot related to daily routine. They both had in mind a box on a corner near the bank, although a little more discretion than to make use of that one should be shown.

Perhaps not, though, Madden reflected. He had brought about the arrest of a number of people who were under the illusion that once they dropped an unsigned letter in the mail it couldn't be traced back to them.

The waitress served his lunch and Rod's coffee. After her departure Rod reported that no one at the post office had noticed mail coming from or addressed to Newton, Pennsylvania. "They never heard of the place," he added.

Madden nodded, devoted himself to his plate for a few minutes, and then asked Rod what he knew about the Blaines.

Rod knew Gibb better than he knew the parents. Gibb, he said, was an all-right guy; not too much on the ball, maybe, but an all-right guy.

He didn't know that Gibb Blaine's name had a place on the list of young men Lucia had dated within the past year. If he had known it, his tone wouldn't have been so impartial, Madden suspected. He was definitely interested in Lucia Ruyter.

"Kind of a funny guy, really, when you stop to think about it," Rod continued. "Studious and inclined to keep to himself. When he was a kid in high school he used to be in and out of the post office a lot. I was a clerk in those days and sold him stamps for his collection."

Madden, a fellow-collector, inquired, "Does he still keep it up?"

"He must. His mother was in buying some for him a few weeks ago. I ran into her in the lobby and we had a little chat. She's very pleasant and not a bad-looking woman for her age. But you've met her yourself, I don't have to tell you about her."

"Well, she was pleasant enough to me," Madden agreed, "but not to her husband. You couldn't miss it that where she sits is the head of the table."

"Alec's the kind of wishy-washy guy who invites that sort of thing," Rod commented. "When I used to be on the windows and she came into the post office, I don't remember her ever saying much about him. She always talked about Gibb, how well he was doing in college and so forth. Lately, of course, it's the wonderful new job in Seattle whenever I run into her."

"Is Gibb Blaine, by any chance, what Lucia would call a square?"

Rod raised his eyebrows in thought, grinned, and replied, "Yes, I guess he is, now that you mention it. He's certainly not what she might describe as a cool cat." After a pause he asked, "But where does Gibb come into your case, Inspector? He's in Seattle and hasn't been home since he went there months ago."

"Lucia dated him last summer. But wasn't, I gathered, much interested."

"Oh." Rod digested this piece of information in silence for a moment and then shook his head. "I wouldn't expect Gibb Blaine to take up poison pen letter writing even if he were right here in Fairmount to do it. I'd say it isn't in him to get that steamed up over a girl."

A mental image of Gibb Blaine's father came into Madden's mind, and he said, "I guess I'll buy that."

He finished his lunch. But he wasn't, he discovered, quite ready to drop the Blaines. He asked Rod what he thought of Alec.

"Well, he's one of the names I checked off on that personnel list you gave me," Rod reminded him. "I never heard anything against him, he seems to get along all right at the bank. Maybe it's being henpecked that makes him so quiet."

"Yes." Meditating aloud, Madden added, "I wonder what other effect years and years of it would have on a man."

Rod stared at him. "I don't know," he said. "I suppose it could be that you'd find some way to break loose sooner or later. But with Alec, not by writing the letters. There's too much kindness in him to do it. He wouldn't have the guts for it anyway."

Madden, not disposed to challenge this analysis, was now prepared to change the subject. Rod changed it for him by announcing that he was bothered by the tone of the letters Lucia had been getting lately.

"I hope she's keeping in mind what I told her the other night," Madden remarked.

"Oh, she is, all right."

"Good. That gives you a clear field, doesn't it?" Madden offered this comment with a straight face, but Rod caught the twinkle in his eyes and laughed a little sheepishly.

Madden couldn't resist adding, "Just so she doesn't get the idea that it's a cooked-up deal and that I'm running interference on it for you, you should be all set."

He pushed aside his plate, and lit a cigarette. "What did you hear about that hit-and-run thing last fall?"

"Why—" Rod looked at the postal inspector blankly, recovered, and said, "I didn't even know Lucia then. All I heard was what everybody else heard. She was knocked down by a car that didn't stop, and the police never found out whose it was or who was driving it." He paused. "You don't think it was an accident? It was in the papers as one at the time, there wasn't a question of—"

"No, there wouldn't have been. The only reason I question it is that it's something else that's happened to her. There may not be a connection, but first she was knocked down by a hit-and-run driver and was lucky not to have been badly injured or even killed; then, a few months later the letters start, chiefly directed at her. That's why I'm taking a good long look at her accident."

"Yes, and when you put it like that, it makes me take another look at it myself." Rod eyed the inspector worriedly. "What can we do about it?"

"We're already doing what we can," Madden told him. "Lucia's not going out with anyone but you right now, and you're looking out for her. If I went to the police they'd want more than my suspicions before they started another investigation of a case that's entered on their records as a hit-and-run. For that matter, perhaps it was; perhaps it has no connection with the letters at all. The things that bother us in the ones Lucia's been getting lately may be just another twist in the writer's mind."

"How I'd like to get my hands on the bastard," Rod declared in a burst of anger. "When I think of Lucia and the Bauer kid and the other people whose lives are being turned upside down by those lousy letters, I could—"

"You're doing all you can," Madden pointed out.

"I wish I could do more, a lot more." After a pause Rod added, "Everybody I know at the bank, male or female, married or single, keeps running through my head. It's enough to drive you batty trying to figure out which one it could be and never coming up with a name that you can really feel sure of. And then when I talk to Lucia about it I get the same answer every time; she's had no trouble with anyone at the bank, nothing that would start all this. I tried again last night to get it across to her that it could

135

have been something so slight from her point of view that she'd never given it a second thought. But she said no, it couldn't be as slight as that, there must be another motive."

Rod hesitated for a moment. Then he said, "Look, Inspector, I'm not sure she doesn't have ideas of her own on it. For instance, she got talking last night about character and personality and a person's general behavior entering into it. Some people, she said, would be utterly incapable of writing the letters, it simply wasn't in them to do it. Others, she said, might do it for a reason that wouldn't seem valid at all to a normal person. The way she talked made me wonder if she didn't have someone in particular in mind. But when I tried to pin her down on it, I didn't get anywhere. Perhaps you could if you tried."

"I'll drop in on her later today," Madden said. "God knows I'd like to get this case cleared up as soon as I can. I've got an S.I. tour coming up in a couple of weeks."

He looked at his watch. Ten minutes past one. Before Lucia got home from the bank he'd have time to run over to Glenwood, the next town, and have a talk with the postmaster about the proposed renovation of the Glenwood post office.

She should be home by four-thirty. Then he'd try to find out whose character and personality she thought might lead to the letters.

As he drove to Glenwood he examined some of his own views on the subject. Inez Blaine fitted right into the pattern they formed.

Chapter Thirteen

Lucia said in a tone that betrayed her annoyance, "Doesn't Rod have anything better to do with his time than run to you with my thoughts on people?"

Madden, wanting to keep Rod out of it, had tried to persuade her that in one of her conversations with him she had given him the impression that there was someone she suspected. But Lucia brushed this pretense aside. Just last night the subject had come up with Rod, not Madden; she hadn't seen the latter in the past few days while so much of her thinking had been concentrated on it.

She continued, "Rod and I were talking, and I simply said I thought some people were capable of doing awful things whereas others, you know instinctively, would never do them, regardless of the provocation."

Madden settled back in his chair in Lucia's living room. It was after five o'clock, the room a little shadowy. She stood up to turn on a light and at the same time cut down the volume of a radio program of piano selections to a whisper of sound.

When she was back in her chair he said, "I'm an outsider in this. I could use your help in figuring out these people." He smiled at her. "You know, sheep from goats, wheat from chaff."

He waited. He wasn't ready to bring in Inez Blaine's name himself. He wanted to know if Lucia's suspicions coincided with his.

She said, "I'd love to be able to help, Inspector, but how can I when I have nothing but my thoughts about whether this one or that one would be capable of writing the letters? On that basis, it isn't fair to bring in names."

"The letters aren't what you'd call fair either," he reminded her dryly. "Look at the misery they've caused, the lives they've upset. Look at the Bauer kid wandering around God knows where and liable to get into all kinds of trouble. Any ideas you have that would—"

Lucia broke in. "But just because I don't like someone—how could I start airing what are nothing more than prejudices?"

"Why not?" Madden demanded. He stood up and began to walk around the room. "What do you think would happen if you did? Do you expect me to rush out and tell the whole town about it?"

"Well . . ." She looked at him helplessly.

He pressed his point. "Whatever you tell me will be just between us. I'll decide for myself if there's anything in it or not. If there isn't, what harm is done? If there is, it will be a faster step forward in nailing the one we're looking for. Sooner or later," he concluded purposefully, "I intend to nail that person anyway. With the benefit of what you know about these people, things that it takes an outsider time to learn, it might be sooner, that's all."

Lucia was wavering. "If only I had a few facts . . ."

"I'm not asking for facts. I'm only asking you to—" Madden stopped short, swinging around to the radio as he caught what the announcer who had interrupted a Mozart selection was saying. ". . . crashed near West-bridge shortly after its take-off from Lomas Field . . ."

He turned up the volume, and the announcer's voice

138

came in resonant and clear. "It is not yet known if there are any survivors."

Madden waited to hear no more. Reaching for his hat and coat, he said to Lucia, "I've got to leave right away. There'll be mail on that plane."

He was gone before she could reply, his car already moving away by the time she collected herself and looked out the front window.

The car radio turned on as he drove to Dunston, Madden picked up one more news bulletin on the crash. The plane, an Interstate airliner, had taken off from Lomas Field at four-thirty on a scheduled flight to Chicago. Radio contact had been lost soon after its take-off, and the next news of its whereabouts had come from a farmer who telephoned the police at Westbridge, Connecticut, that he had just seen a plane crash into the side of Steeple Mountain. There was still no information available as to whether or not any of the fifty-two passengers aboard had survived the crash. Police and airline officials were now on their way to the scene, and further details would be released as soon as possible.

Westbridge was in Madden's territory. Responsibility for recovering mail aboard the plane rested primarily on him, although other inspectors in the Dunston office could be expected to assist him.

He drove as fast as conditions allowed, his side of the road fairly clear with most of the traffic coming out of Dunston, not going toward it.

When he reached the Dunston Federal Building he stopped first at the loading platform to commandeer a truck, mail pouches, electric lanterns, and flashlights and to deputize the driver who would accompany him. Then he took the elevator up to his office. It was nearly six o'clock and the only inspector waiting there for him was Palmisano, who was on the phone reporting the crash to Division Headquarters in Boston. When

139

Madden entered the room, Palmisano said over his shoulder that he'd heard about it just a few minutes ago as he was getting ready to leave for the day.

A few minutes later they were in the truck and heading first for the airport. The driver talked a little, neither of the inspectors had much to say. They knew what lay ahead of them, the driver didn't.

At Lomas Field a crowd had already collected, but the police were maintaining order holding back the curiosity seekers who had no business there. The inspectors left the driver to find a parking space and separated inside the airport building, Palmisano starting for the air-mail field office to get a copy of the mail manifest and list of registered pieces, Madden going to the operations office, and finally, by means of his identification folder, breaking through lesser employees to reach the manager. The latter, white with strain, took him into the operations room and on the big wall map pointed out the area in which the plane was reported to have crashed.

Soon thereafter the inspectors were back in the truck studying a road map, picking out what they thought would be the quickest route to Westbridge, although not the shortest in actual count of miles. The main roads were the shortest, but at this hour clogged with homegoing traffic. They chose to follow back roads where there was little traffic, stopping only at a roadside stand for sandwiches and coffee.

By eight-thirty they were in Westbridge, halting the one patrolman in sight in that smallish town to ask the way to Steeple Mountain. Follow the road they were on straight out of town, he told them. Bear left at the first intersection beyond it. That would take them up a hill to a dirt road on their left, the only one leading to the scene of the crash.

"You won't have no trouble finding it once you get up

140

on the hill," the patrolman added. "They got roadblocks set up around the whole area."

Clear of the town, climbing the hill, they could see a reddish glow in the sky to the west, barely visible through the mist that had begun to roll in around them half an hour earlier. As they reached the top of the hill a fine drizzle began to fall, leading Madden to observe, "Ever notice how things like this go? They're not bad enough in themselves, there's got to be something extra thrown in. It rains or it snows or some other damn thing happens to make it still rougher."

"'Neither snow nor rain nor heat nor gloom of night,'" Palmisano reminded him with a grin.

A mile farther on they began to pass cars parked on both sides of the road with people standing around them staring at the glow in the west, the dimly seen outline of the range of hills. A state police car stopped them after they had covered another mile, one of the troopers getting out to examine their identification before waving them on.

At the beginning of the dirt road that led up Steeple Mountain a roadblock had been set up by state and Westbridge police, whose uniformed figures stood out against the flickering light of the flares.

The inspectors learned from them that Interstate's rescue crew had arrived a short time ago but so far had found no survivors. Wreckage of the plane was scattered all over the side of the mountain. No reports had come in yet of recovered mail. Representatives of the Railway Express Agency had gone up the mountain ahead of them, bound on an errand like their own.

"They just left here," a state trooper remarked. "You'll find them right up ahead."

Floodlights brightened the misty blackness of the night as they talked with the officers. "They finally got them working," someone said. A helicopter zigzagged back and forth across the area dropping flares, and then the drone of a low-flying plane could be heard. "CAP," a state trooper said as Madden glanced skyward.

"How close can we get with the truck?" the latter asked.

"They're parking in a field up there about a mile from where the nose of the plane hit. That's as close as you'll be able to get, Inspector."

Madden thanked the trooper, they climbed back in the truck and started up the dirt road that curved along the mountainside. Another floodlight was turned on and now they could see the nose of the plane, still burning, silhouetted against a ridge, and far off to the left of it, almost hidden by trees, the lesser glow from some other part of the plane.

Soon they rounded a bend in the road and saw ahead of them a floodlit field choked with cars and trucks that spilled over into the yard of the farmhouse beyond it. Here the road sloped away from the tangle of trees and underbrush that marked the crash area which they could reach only on foot.

They found a place to park the truck and made their way through a melee of fire engines, press cars, civil defense cars, ambulances, doctors' cars, police cars, and others unidentifiable to a state trooper standing in the farmyard. He told them that some mail had been collected by airline personnel and was in the charge of a civil defense worker somewhere up ahead near the wreckage.

Another civil defense worker stepped forward, volunteering the information that he'd heard there was a lot of mail scattered through some fields a couple of miles to the north. Then a Railway Express Company agent joined them with the suggestion that they form a skirmish line and fan out from it to hunt for mail and express packages at the same time.

This was the start of a night that Madden did not care afterward to remember. The drizzle turned into a sleety downpour, and outside the range of the lights each man carried lay murky darkness that gave no warning of thorny underbrush, fences, boulders, barbed wire, and swamps through which they plowed their way under the guidance of a civil defense worker to the spot where the tail section of a the plane rested partly buried in the ground. Here Madden recovered two torn mail sacks from the man guarding them, and here he and the others formed their line of search.

They were wet through by this time and chilled by the wind that whipped across the mountain. They followed the path of the plane by the pieces that had sprayed out from it as it disintegrated, some of them gouging deep holes in the ground. There was blood and something else on the first mail pouch Madden found, the lock twisted off and letters scattered like snow around it. He felt sick for a while after that, and then tears stung his eyes unexpectedly when he came upon a baby's nursing bottle, the nipple still on it, lying in his path. He saw remnants of bodies here and there along the way. He found mail, some of it undamaged, some torn, some charred to fragments, all of it finding a place in the pouches he carried.

Sometime during the night he approached what at first appeared to be the intact body of a woman. But when he drew closer he saw that it was her wool suit that held her together. . . .

The mountainside was dotted with the lights of search parties and below he could hear car motors start up and die away in the distance, although the downpour and murk kept him from seeing their lights. Somewhere far off a dog howled steadily as if in protest at this gruesome horror.

He passed a pocketbook caught on a bush, a motor buried except for one blade of the propeller. He picked up an express company package, the box torn, the doll inside miraculously whole. He mentioned the body he had seen to a search party he met. Eventually, after midnight, he reached what was left of the nose of the plane, a thin column of smoke still rising from it in spite of the rain and the chemicals the firemen had poured on it. Someone thrust a paper cup of coffee into his hand and he drank it gratefully, but could not touch the sandwich that was offered with it, with the stench of death around him and the memory of the things he had seen that night.

Presently Palmisano, the mail truck driver, and the express company agents straggled in one by one as soaked, weary, and downhearted as he. Madden checked the recovered mail against the manifest in the flood-lighted area that was as bright as day, too bright, sparing them nothing of the scene. Out of twenty-eight pouches listed on the manifest they had recovered in whole or part something under fifteen. They would have to follow up the story they'd heard when they first arrived of mail scattered through fields to the north. But there wasn't going to be enough of it to make up the balance missing. They would have to search the area already covered by daylight, although they couldn't, Madden said, have missed that much of it.

"Some of it's burned up completely or buried under pieces of wreckage," he said. "We won't know how much until they bring in a crane."

They went down the mountain to the farm where they'd left the truck, and with a police officer acting as guide drove to the fields where more mail had been reported. They found it loose, blown about in the mud,

144

plastered against bushes, caught in crevices of stone walls, close to two full pouches of it, Madden estimated, when they reassembled at the truck over an hour later.

"We'll go back to Westbridge and weigh what we've got," he said.

The town being in his territory, he knew the postmaster. It was quarter of three on a cold sleety morning, but after the night he had spent Madden had little compunction over getting the postmaster out of bed to open the post office.

He phoned him from a highway booth, the postmaster answering on the first ring. He'd been expecting a call, he said, and hadn't undressed, lying down on a sofa while he waited to hear from the inspector. He'd meet them at the post office right away.

He lived near it and was there ahead of them with the heat turned on and thermos bottles of hot soup and coffee prepared by his wife.

Madden dropped down on a chair in the workroom and let Palmisano and the truck driver, younger men, taking the night better than he, help the postmaster weigh the mail they had collected.

When the weighing was done one hundred and thirty pounds of the mail were still unaccounted for, but it would have to wait for daylight. Bone-weary, Madden sat in his chair letting the warmth invade his cold wet body while he alternated swallows of soup and coffee. Finally he said with the least smile lighting his dark face, "It's just possible that I'll survive this. A little while ago I didn't think I would."

It was almost three-thirty, too late to drive to Dunston where they would only have to turn around and come back after an hour or two. The postmaster took them home with him, offering twin beds in the room that belonged to a son away at college and a sofa in the living room. They spread their clothes out near radiators to dry and slept until the postmaster's wife awakened them at seven o'clock for breakfast, she deploring the fact that they couldn't get more rest before going out to renew the search for mail.

It had stopped raining, but by daylight the scene was even worse. There was something obscene, Madden thought, about the path of desolation the plane had left in its wake, the broken twisted wreckage it had become, the havoc it had created.

They recovered two more sacks of mail that morning along with a great many loose pieces. A civil defense worker turned over several pieces to Madden, who glanced through it to note its condition before dropping it in a pouch. "Mr. Gilbert Blaine" typed on a mud-stained envelope leaped to his eye, then the Seattle address, Fairmount return address. Excitement stirred in him. Streaked and stained though the envelope was, he had seen other examples of the typing on it too often lately not to recognize it at once.

His glance went again to the return address. No name was included to tell him which of the Blaines had written it. But he felt quite sure that it was Inez.

This was a wonderful piece of luck, he exulted to himself. Not so much that the letter had been on the plane—Inez Blaine probably wrote air mail to her son every day—but that it had been found loose instead of in a sack and turned over to him instead of Palmisano or the truck driver who would have no reason to give it a second glance.

Madden put the letter in an inside pocket and went on with the search, his thoughts on his find and the best use he could make of it.

He couldn't hold it up or photostat it; that would be illegal. With the envelope clearly intact he couldn't even open it to make assurance doubly sure by looking at the signature. He'd have to try, through a Seattle inspector, to get the letter back after it had been delivered to Gibb Blaine.

When he found himself alone with Palmisano he discussed ways and means with him.

"If I have a Seattle inspector deliver it with a story about needing it back as evidence in the plane crash, Blaine would probably hand it over after he'd read it," Madden said. "But I don't think that will do. He'd sure as hell give the alarm by writing home about it. I can't have that. His letter isn't enough by itself. Until I get some airtight evidence, I don't want to risk drying up the source of supply."

"What about fishing it out of the rubbish?" Palmisano suggested. "I don't imagine the guy saves letters from home tied up with a pink ribbon. He'll keep it around, maybe, until he's answered it and then tear it across a couple of times and drop it in a wastebasket. He's got an apartment, you say, so the janitor can be alerted to keep his trash separate."

"The Seattle inspector will love that assignment, pawing through somebody's trash." Madden laughed at the picture he conjured. "But it's a better idea than mine. Let's hope Blaine doesn't have an apartment in some old house with fireplaces."

"Don't be so pessimistic," said Palmisano, and they went back to work.

By noon a crane had been brought in. When the wreckage of the nose was lifted nearly a hundred pounds of mail was found underneath it, most of it in fairly good condition. At two o'clock Madden computed the total and discovered that it came very close to checking with the manifest. Since the whole area had been secured from sightseers, whatever stray piece of mail they'd missed would be found by workers and handed in at the Westbridge post office. His job here was done, he could leave now with Palmisano and the truck driver.

At the Dunston post office he arranged to put a detail of clerks on the recovered mail, most of which had already been dried out in Westbridge. It would be the clerk's task to sort it out, decipher as many addresses as they could and forward the mail, returning it to senders whenever possible if the addressees were indecipherable.

After he had parted reluctantly with Gibb Blaine's letter Madden went up to his office, phoned in a report on the recovered mail to Division Headquarters, and then put in a person-to-person call to the inspector in charge in Seattle, eventually reaching him at home, this being Saturday afternoon. Madden asked to have a cover put on Gibb Blaine's mail until the air-mail letter arrived, described it carefully, and proceeded to outline his plan for getting it back. The Seattle man laughed, said he'd take care of the mail cover right away, and put an inspector on operation trash as soon as the letter arrived.

Madden thanked him and hung up. It was now nearly six o'clock. He went home to his apartment, took a hot shower, fell into bed, and slept through until nine o'clock Sunday morning.

He went out to breakfast, bought a paper, and read what it said about the plane crash that hadn't made quite such big headlines on this, the second day after the occurrence. It wasn't until he was back in his apartment that he remembered he had been invited out to dinner today and that he himself had invited Ann Lanier, a lady he had met recently, out to dinner last night and had stood her up cold.

Appalled at his memory lapse, he went to the phone to make what amends he could by explaining what had happened and issuing another invitation.

The lady proved to be sympathetic and understanding.

When he hung up Madden felt he was reassembling his life again, and for the first time since he'd heard of the plane crash he wondered if there had been any new developments in Fairmount since he'd left Lucia in a pell-mell rush Friday afternoon.

He would find out tomorrow.

Chapter Fourteen

Late that Sunday night Frieda Bauer was picked up by Baltimore, Maryland, police while trying to hitch a ride, destination Florida, where, she told police, she hoped to get a job as a waitress in one of the resort areas.

Madden heard this on the eight o'clock news broadcast Monday morning and that the girl's father had left for Baltimore to bring her home. He speculated on what would happen when father and daughter met; if days of not knowing what had become of her had brought about a change in the father's attitude. From what he had seen of the man he doubted it, thought it more likely that Fred Bauer would give her a hard time over what she had done. Even if he didn't, there would still be permanent scars for the whole family, a question mark in the minds of Fairmount townspeople concerning Frieda Bauer, a tendency on the part of mothers to prefer not to have their sons go out with her. She could be considered a major casualty of the letters, Madden thought.

He called Rod Harrison as soon as he reached his office, and learned that the pattern held with no letters mailed over the week end.

"Well, this is Monday, there should be something today," the inspector said. "I've got a pretty full schedule but I'll be out sometime this afternoon, in time for the night collection anyway. It's going to be interesting to see what it turns up."

After he had talked with Rod he gave his attention to his mail, skimming through reports of losses, a list of personnel changes, a notice on a check forger working the country, a letter from Division Headquarters on a survey of carrier needs he had sent in. Sorting through the rest, he picked out a letter from the Pittsburgh inspector assigned to the inquiries Madden had asked for in Newton.

It began with a summary of the indecent assault case that differed in no substantial way from the story Ben Davidson had related himself. The next paragraph informed Madden that the Newton postmaster had no record of a change of address to a Connecticut town within the regulation two years that such records were kept. The postmaster, who said he was able to keep in touch with nearly everyone in Newton, further asserted that he could recall no one having moved to Connecticut within the past several years. Nor did he know of anyone who corresponded with friends or relatives in the Fairmount area.

The Pittsburgh inspector closed with the statement that if he could be further assistance Madden had only to call on him.

Madden put aside the letter in chagrin. He had counted on being given the name of someone who had moved from Newton to a city or town in the Fairmount area. That had seemed to him the likeliest way for the Davidson story to have reached anyone in Fairmount. Anyone? Inez Blaine. Although he wouldn't put all of his eggs in that basket just yet.

Right now he had to consider how else the story could have gotten out. He sat back from his desk discarding, after due thought, the prospect of Inez or anyone else hearing it through some business association or during an overnight stop in Newton on a pleasure trip.

How else could it have happened? Was there a private school or college in Newton or nearby that someone from Fairmount—Gibb Blaine—could have attended? A new summer camp opened in recent years?

He reached for his phone and called the reference room of the Dunston library. Within a few minutes he found out there were no private schools, colleges, or summer camps in or near Newton.

He got up from his desk, walked across the room and back, fidgeted with a window blind, sat down again. There had to be some way to put two people together, one from Newton, one from Fairmount, long enough to build up an acquaintance that would lead to gossip about Davidson. His name would have had to come up in an incidental fashion. He'd never lived in Newton and had worked there only two summers at the camp. Being a young man then, he would have made it his business to meet Newton girls. Had one of them, a middle-aged woman now, remembered him after all these years? Or had it been a man, young himself at the time, and perhaps jealous of Davidson over some girl? There must have been something like that to fix Davidson in some Newton person's memory. Then his name came up in conversation and the old scandal was revived.

Madden could almost hear the conversation. "Yes, it must be the same man. . . ." The description given, the comparing of notes. "Yes, I heard he got a job with a bank in Connecticut after he finished college. . . ."

A thing like that hadn't come out during an overnight stay in Newton on a vacation trip.

Vacation trip. Madden examined the words. Vacation trip, vacation. Cut himself loose from Newton, place the meeting somewhere else. Where could the preliminary gossipy relationship have been built up? Not on the road,

153

not enough leisure for talk.

Vacation resort, he thought next. Too remote a possibility? No, not really, not any more remote than anything else that had occurred to him. At least worth a try.

He reached for the phone, called Rod, and asked if he knew where the Blaines went on their vacation last summer.

"The Blaines?" After a moment of startled silence, Rod said, "Bar Harbor, I think. They go there every summer."

"Do you know if they were away over Christmas?"

"I'm sure they weren't. I met her around New Year's and she said the holidays hadn't been the same without Gibb, and how much they'd missed not having him home and so on."

"Oh. Then it's Bar Harbor." Madden thanked him and hung up. He rang for the stenographer and dictated an air-mail letter to the Pittsburgh inspector, asking him to have the Newton postmaster make up as soon as possible a list of Newton people, all that he could remember, who'd had mail forwarded while on vacation and the resorts to which it had been sent.

In a small place like Newton, Madden thought, the postmaster, checking around and drawing on his own memory, might come up with a list that was fairly complete.

Madden had just finished dictating his letter to Pittsburgh when a young man who had made a ten o'clock appointment arrived to pour out his troubles.

He was engaged, he said, and planned to be married in the spring. But there was another girl who wanted him to marry her. It took Madden some time to extract this information from him, the young man protesting over and over that Madden wasn't to think he considered himself anything so special that the other girl should be

154

on his neck, but, still, that was how it was. She said she was in love with him and was bombarding him at his office and home with letters proclaiming the fact, and demanding that he break his engagement and marry her. What made it particularly difficult was that now she'd also started writing to his fiancée saying she must release him so that he could marry her.

He'd explained to his fiancée that the other girl was wacky—"She must be," he interjected with a self-deprecating grin, "chasing me like this"—but it had become so embarrassing he didn't know what to do and needed Madden's help.

Madden asked if the letters were threatening in any way. No, they weren't. Nor scurrilous, nor obscene, nor defamatory. Just embarrassing as hell, the young man said. And a great nuisance.

He finally produced the most recent effusions. And there was, after all, a threat of sorts in one of them. "I can't bear to lose you," a paragraph ran. "I can't live without you. If you won't change your mind, I'll come to Dunston next week and wait outside your office for you every day just to tell you how much I love you and what a terrible mistake you made when you threw me over. There's no one in the world who'll ever love you the way I do, my darling belovedest."

"So you see," the young man said when Madden handed back the letters, "I've got to get her off my neck. I can't have her arriving at my office next week and making scenes in front of everyone."

He looked desperate. The inspector had to exercise the sternest self-control not to laugh as he took down the girl's name and address and promised to see her and do what he could to abate the nuisance of her unwelcome attentions.

"Of course there's no law that says you can't write love letters to people who don't want to receive them," he pointed out. "But I'll have a talk with her anyway. If it does no good and she lands at your office next week and starts making scenes, I guess you'll just have to call the police."

"Oh, my God," the young man said in despair. "But you will try to talk her out of it?"

"I certainly will," Madden assured him and sent him on his way a little comforted.

His next appointment was with an elderly lady who complained that the neighbors were stealing her mail. This, the inspector's questions brought out, boiled down to a single incident, that of a neighbor in the next apartment who had offered to bring up her mail and had later come back with a letter of the elderly lady's which she said had gotten mixed up with her own mail. No, it hadn't shown signs of being tampered with, but there were ways of doing it so that it wouldn't show, weren't there? Such an important letter too. And so on.

Madden's next appointment was with a man who had a legitimate complaint about merchandise ordered from a mail-order house, paid for, and not what the advertisement represented it to be when it arrived. The man was excitable, and getting the details of his complaint straightened out took twice as long as it should have. Other appointments, other demands on Madden's time followed, and in the end it was nearly three o'clock when he reached Fairmount.

He stopped first at the bank and saw Ben Davidson, who looked astonished when asked what girls he had gone out with in Newton over twenty-three years ago. He rallied, exercised his memory, and came up with a girl named May. No matter how he tried he couldn't supply her last name. Just May and that she had dark hair and eyes, which meager information would, Madden said, get them nowhere.

A rival for her affections? Ben Davidson could recall none.

That was that. The inspector left him to wrestle with his fragmentary memories and sought out Mr. Hasbrouck, who told him that no bank employee, other than those he already knew about, had admitted receiving one of the letters.

He wasn't surprised to learn this. Nothing was going right today.

Mr. Hasbrouck's secretary had prepared a list of typewriters owned by employees. So far her inquiries had established a total of twelve, one of them a Smith Corona but not a portable. Also turned over to Madden were typing samples from six machines, none of it bearing much similarity to that in the letters.

"There must be other typewriters, though," Mr. Hasbrouck said. "We'll keep after it."

"Fine," Madden said.

Mr. Hasbrouck, with Mr. Jenner invisible but undoubtedly hovering over him, manfully concealed his disappointment that Madden himself had nothing definite to report. He turned the conversation to the Bauers, remarking on what a relief it must be to the parents to have the daughter located. Madden agreed and said good-by to him.

Pausing outside the bank president's office, he glanced in Lucia's direction. Although many of her fellow-workers were preparing to leave for the day, she was still busy at her desk and didn't notice him. He would see her later, he decided—after the night collection of the mail.

It was four-thirty when he emerged from the bank. It would soon be time for the night collection to begin. He drove to the post office.

Rod, expecting his arrival, announced that the superintendent of mails was going out with the driver and

157

would look through the mail as it was removed from each box.

Seated in the postmaster's office with him, the inspector, without going into details or mentioning Ben Davidson by name, told Rod about the contact with Newton that must exist and his own thoughts on it.

"I guess it's a pretty thin lead," he concluded, "but I can't come up with a better one at the moment."

"It may not be so thin after all," Rod said. "If Newton's such a small place, the postmaster may have a pretty good list for you." After a pause he added, "The Blaines did go to Bar Harbor last summer. In August. I asked a question here and there this afternoon just to make sure."

"Oh. Well, I didn't mention Bar Harbor to the Pittsburgh inspector. I thought I might as well get all the information I could without limiting myself to one place."

Madden went on to tell him about the letter found after the plane crash and the steps he had taken to get it back.

A long discussion of Inez Blaine followed. Rod at first inclined to disbelief that she could be involved in the case, but eventually delving deep in his memory and coming up with various small things that didn't fit in with the public image she had created of herself.

They went out for coffee. It was well after six o'clock when they got back to the post office.

Presently the superintendent of mails came in with two letters in his hand. He handed them to Madden, saying, "I think these are what you're looking for, Inspector."

A glance at the typing so familiar by this time that he felt as if he could pick it out in the dark told Madden that here were two more of the letters, one addressed to Lucia, the other to Inez Blaine.

"Yes," he said. "What box were they in?"

"The one outside the Fairmount Pharmacy."

"Oh. That's right in the Center, isn't it?"

"Yes. It gets a lot of use."

Madden thanked the superintendent, who went back to the workroom. Rod said, "It's a combination box, used as a relay box too. It's cleared several times a day."

He went on to explain that the last clearing before the night collection was made between two-thirty and three o'clock by one of the carriers on his way back to the post office. If the letters were mailed regularly in that box, it was between the time of the last clearing by a carrier and the time when the truck making the night collection would reach it. Ordinarily, this would be about quarter of six. Tonight, of course, Rod continued, the time schedule had been considerably off with the delay caused by keeping the collection from each box separate.

It was seven o'clock. Rod went out into the workroom, ran the two letters through the canceling machine, and brought them back to the inspector, who said he would deliver them himself. Then he said, "By the way, talking to Lucia the other day I tried to keep you out of it but she wouldn't have it that way. Did she say anything to you about it?"

"Yes, but that was after she'd had time to think it over. She said she realized we were both just doing our job."

"Good." Madden added with exaggerated concern, "The last thing I'd want to do would be to throw a monkey wrench in the path of—uh—shall I call it true love?"

"Call it whatever you like, Inspector." Rod's face reddened, his tone dismissed the subject.

Madden laughed and turned to the telephone, reflecting that Rod must be badly smitten when he couldn't take even a little kidding about Lucia.

He dialed her number. There was no answer, although he let it ring and ring. Then Rod remembered that she'd been invited to dinner tonight by some girl at the bank.

"I'll try her later," Madden said, and looked up the Blaines' number.

Alec Blaine answered the phone. His wife wasn't home, he said. She'd gone to a dinner meeting of the nursing board but should be home before nine. Madden said he would drop by then, hung up and looked at his watch. He would have time for a leisurely dinner before he saw the Blaines.

He arrived at their house at quarter of nine. Alec admitted him, announcing that his wife hadn't come home yet but should be there any minute.

Madden followed him into the living room, sat down, and made himself comfortable while the older man perched on the edge of a chair, his pale blue eyes fixed apprehensively on the postal inspector.

"I saw you with Mr. Hasbrouck today," he said. "Is there—more trouble?"

"Well, two more letters, one of them addressed to your wife. I brought it along to her."

"Oh," Alec said. "Oh . . ." And next, "I hope—the other one upset her terribly although she pretended to you that it didn't." He leaned forward, his glance seeking a reprieve. "It seems too bad she has to be upset again."

"I'm afraid a letter can't be withheld from the addressee, Mr. Blaine."

"I suppose not." A look of resignation settled on his face. "It's just that—well, perhaps you wouldn't know it to look at her, Inspector, but my wife feels things more than she shows. Everything. Like Gibb taking that job in Seattle. She hasn't been herself since he left. And now there're the letters about poor Miss Ross and me. It's not that she doesn't trust me. I know she does. Implicitly.

But letters like that would upset anyone, they . . ." His voice trickled away into silence.

Madden made no reply. His voice would have given away his thoughts on Inez Blaine's sadistic treatment of her husband.

Out from under her influence, he was proving to be unexpectedly talkative, nervous, probably, over the prospect of his wife's reaction to another letter.

He contined, "She'll come home wanting to tell me all about the board meeting—she does seem to enjoy her work with the VNA—and then the letter will spoil the whole thing for her. It's too bad."

"Yes," Madden said, and added a moment later, "I understand she does quite a bit of civic work. It must keep her busy."

"It does. She gives a lot of time to it. More than ever since Gibb went away. If she stays home, she says, she just mopes and thinks about him and how far away from her he is."

Alec Blaine's voice held no particular note, and yet it told of coming home to an empty house to prepare his own meals, of long hours alone while his wife pursued her own interests.

Fed her own ego by gaining civic prominence, Madden reflected, not prepared to credit her with being truly public-spirited or possessing any other worth-while trait.

"She's particularly interested in the VNA," Alec offered next. "She always says it's her pet agency."

"What kind of work does she do there?"

"Everything. I've heard her say, from diapering babies at Well Child Conferences to letting people weep on her shoulder while she types their case histories. The budget doesn't permit paid office help, you see, so they all have to pitch in to get things done." After a pause Alec Blaine added, "I shouldn't say all, though. My wife complains that the other volunteers don't show up half the time or do their share."

Madden moved slightly, was still again. He said, "They're supposed to be there certain hours each week?"

"Yes, but—" The older man broke off as lights flashed across the front windows from a car turning in at the driveway. "My wife," he said.

Inez Blaine came in and greeted Madden, remarking, "I wondered whose car was out front." Then she handed her keys to her husband and said, "Will you put the car away, Alec? There's the worst clutter blocking the garage."

He seemed to retreat into himself with her arrival. "Clutter?" he said. "I don't know what it could be."

"Oh, rubbish cans and things."

"But they're off to the side, they're not—"

"Heaven's sake, Alec, will you put the car away or won't you? We don't want to involve the inspector in a family dispute."

The laugh she gave had an edged note in it. Her husband said no more but went out to put the car away.

While he was gone Inez removed her outdoor things, sat down, and said, "Older houses are a nuisance. Garages separate and away out in back. Imagine. In this day and age. I keep tellling Alec we must get rid of this place, build something more up-to-date."

"Your house seems very comfortable to me," Madden commented, making an effort to keep his feeling toward her out of his voice but finding it difficult, particularly so at the end of a working day now twelve hours long.

"It's out of the ark, Inspector, it really is." She lit a cigarette and suddenly favored him with a gracious smile as if she had become aware of and meant to dispel the reserve in his manner. "But Alec won't see it. He just talks about how much new houses cost these days."

"They run into money," Madden said.

"By the way," she continued, "how is your investigation coming along, Inspector?"

Ignoring the question, he reached in his pocket and brought out her letter. "This was mailed to you today, Mrs. Blaine."

"Today? Then how—? Oh, they found it at the post office? They're looking for them now?"

"Someone happened to notice it while the mail was being sorted."

"Oh, I see." She sighed as she opened the letter. "I suppose this will be more of that horrible nonsense about my husband and Miss Ross."

She read the letter and handed it to Madden. "Yes, it is," she said. "Disgusting."

It was, Madden thought as he read it. But very general with no dates mentioned for the alleged meetings between Miss Ross and Alec Blaine; as in the letter sent to the bank officials, what it said could do him no damage—except with his wife.

"Whoever's doing it," Mrs. Blaine remarked, "doesn't seem to be stopped by the fact that you're making an investigation, Inspector. It's rather a challenge to you, isn't it?"

"It's something more than that," he replied. "It's a violation of federal laws governing the mails."

"Well, you represent the law, don't you?"

"Yes." He read mockery into her air of earnest inquiry.

It was there, but it brought little satisfaction to Inez Blaine just then. Fury had consumed her since midway through the board dinner when she'd heard two of the board members talking about Hetty Davidson's bridge party last week. They'd attended it, and from what they said so had Lucia. Inez hadn't been invited. Hetty

163

Davidson never invited her to the small informal parties she gave. Didn't think Inez was good enough, of course. Well, she'd find out differently before long! When Inez got through with her no one would be caught dead at one of her parties. Except Lucia Ruyter who'd be in the same boat with her.

The thought of Lucia brought up the problem that gnawed at her these days. How could she get stories about the girl started at the bank without having them traced back to her? She'd keep on with the letters, make her next one to Dick Hasbrouck something that would stand what hair he had on end, but they weren't enough, it seemed, to bring the simpleton out of his trance over Lucia. If only she could think of some safe way to start people talking. . . .

Inez became conscious of Madden's gaze resting on her and said with a bright smile, "Your work must be very interesting, Inspector. You run into all kinds of people, don't you?"

"Oh yes," he replied. "All kinds."

Alec Blaine came in, putting an end to this exchange. His face took on a look of hopelessness when Inez informed him that the letter had more to say about his meetings with Lila Ross.

Madden didn't miss the forgiving note in her voice. A turn of the screw, he thought.

She said he could take the letter with him. "I'm sure I don't want such a nasty thing around," she added. "As if I'd believe the lies in it! I guess I know my own husband better than that."

She smiled at the poor wretch, who sat in silence knowing that after Madden was gone he would be put through the wringer once more, would have to explain over and over that he had no idea why he and Lila Ross were attacked, that he'd never looked at her twice, and so

164

on until his wife had reduced him to a pulp. . . .

Madden was glad to say good night and leave.

He drove to Lucia's. Lights were on in her apartment, and when she admitted him she said she had gotten home only a few minutes ago, and no, she hadn't seen Rod or heard from him since last night.

"He's probably tried to call you," Madden told her. "You have another letter." He took it out of his pocket.

"Oh." She looked at the letter without touching it and shook her head. "You read it, please. I think it's about time I gave it up."

The inspector opened and read it, a diatribe of hate directed at Lucia in gutter language, that did not, this time, include threats, actual or implied.

She watched him gravely while he read, but kept her tone light as she inquired, "Well, does it say I'm going to get slugged or something if I don't change my evil ways?"

"No, nothing like that," he answered, relieved at the omission.

Belatedly, Lucia realized that she had kept him standing since he entered the room. She said she was sorry, asked him to sit down, and sat down herself, turning an apologetic gaze on him.

"I've been thinking about the attitude I took last Friday," she said. "It was an extreme form of trying to be fair, I guess. I should have told you right away that the man I think might be capable of writing the letters is Calvin Eads at the bank."

It took Madden a moment to summon a picture of Calvin Eads. "For God's sake," he thought, "that fat, hard-drinking slug?"

Lucia went on, "I can't bear him myself and that's why I worried about being fair to him. He has a slimy way of looking at you sometimes, and drinks a lot and loves to make remarks that have a double meaning. I kept studying him the other day and I decided he's just the type that would enjoy writing the letters."

Madden had wondered if she had at last come to suspect Inez Blaine. But now he recognized that she had blocked herself off from suspecting a woman. She couldn't conceive of one writing such obscenities.

He tried to let her down gently. "Does Eads own a typewriter?"

"I don't know. But you've had Mrs. Cummings inquiring about them at the bank, haven't you? She can find out, I should think, or perhaps I can find out myself."

"His name isn't on the list she gave me."

Lucia eyed the inspector. "You don't think it's Cal, do you?"

"I'll have to look into it before I'm ready to offer an opinion."

She wasn't to be put off that way. She said with a crestfallen expression, "Oh dear, now I feel like a fool. The fuss I made Friday turns out to be much ado about nothing."

"Not necessarily." To ease her discomfiture, Madden went on, "I'm going to tell you in confidence that I'm looking for a Smith Corona portable. If you hear of anyone who owns one, let me know, won't you?"

Lucia said she would, but still looked crestfallen as she said good night.

Driving back to Dunston, the postal inspector thought about Inez Blaine. If he could empty her mind out on a table and examine its contents, what would he find? Sense of persecution, of old scores to be paid back, certainly that. And wasn't her contempt for her husband tied in with her abnormal sense of identification with her son? Probably. She saw him as exclusively hers, an extension of herself.

What else would he find? The usual attitudes of the

poison pen writer, no doubt. The arrogance, the sense of having power over others, the feeling of being above the law, too clever to be caught. All these he'd find in Inez Blaine's mind, and cruelty, envy, and hate. . . .

His thoughts moved on to the typewriter. The chances were that she was using one at the Visiting Nurse Association office, but he would make no move to lay his hands on it yet, not until he had his other evidence assembled, enough of it to weather every defense storm in court.

Chapter Fifteen

The next morning Inspector Madden's aide reported that he had now made the rounds of all but eight of the typewriter agencies in the Dunston area, without uncovering a questionable sale of a Smith Corona portable within the past several months.

Madden told him to go on with his inquiries; the typewriter had to be found and there was, after all, the possibility that he might be wrong in thinking he knew where to find it.

That day and the next he was too busy to go to Fairmount. Wednesday evening, a little before seven, Rod, still at the post office, called Madden at home to tell him one of the letters, addressed to Mrs. Davidson, had been found in the night collection.

"What box?" the inspector asked.

"The same as Monday's. The one outside the pharmacy."

"Oh." Madden glanced out into the kitchen where he had a slice of ham cooking on the range, this being one of the evenings when he had elected to putter over ham and eggs at home and then devote the rest of the evening to his stamp collection, much neglected of late. He held back a sigh and said, "Okay, I'll come out and deliver it tonight. But give Mrs. Davidson a ring to make sure she's home and let me know if she isn't. Otherwise, I'll be out about eight and meet you at the post office."

Rod was waiting for him when he arrived at the post office at eight o'clock, and he sensed immediately the younger man's eagerness to turn over the letter and start him on his way. He was amused, guessing that the reason was a date with Lucia, and co-operated by leaving at once.

On the way to the Davidsons' he mentally composed the words of praise that would go into his final report to the inspector in charge at Division Headquarters for the young assistant postmaster who had given him able and wholehearted assistance in bringing E case 12133 to a successful conclusion with the arrest and imprisonment of the poison pen writer.

He laughed at himself with the reminder that he was nowhere near ready to write that report yet.

Both the Davidsons were home, Ben answering the door and scooping up a baby alligator that crawled across his foot. Tonight the living room was occupied by teenage girls, friends of Jeanie Davidson, playing records. Didn't the senior members of the family ever get the use of it themselves, Madden wondered, as Ben, after he had called his younger son downstairs to retrieve the alligator, took him into the den and closed the door. Mrs. Davidson was there waiting for him in front of the open fire, her greeting friendly but her eyes frightened.

Madden gave her the letter, she read it, first to herself and then aloud. It said:

Dear Mrs. Davidson:

What's it like to be married to a fairy? It must be a strain not to know which sex to be jealous of. But perhaps there is no strain because your husband's never told you about being arrested in Newton, Pennsylvania, in the summer of 1934 after he and

170

another fairy got into a fight. Why don't you ask him to fill you in on all the little details? Better yet, gather the whole family around to hear what he has to say about it. It would make some bedtime story, wouldn't it? Or maybe you'd rather have me write to your children about it. Let me know which way you'd rather have it. Ha, ha, ha!

Mrs. Davidson dropped the letter to her lap and looked at Madden. Her voice shook as she said, "I could not bear it, Inspector, if one of my children ever received a letter like this."

"They won't," he was quick to assure her. "If one should be sent to them it would be delivered to you or your husband just as this one was."

"The vileness of it, though, to even think of telling them, to—" She broke down in tears.

Ben Davidson, his arm around her, tried to offer comfort, telling her that of course the inspector wouldn't let a letter get through to the children; that if by any chance one should get by at the post office they themselves would recognize it for what it was when it was delivered to the house.

"But if they're home when the mail comes, sometimes they bring it in before I know it's there," she wept.

Madden said on a quietly emphatic note, "There isn't going to be a slip-up, Mrs. Davidson. None of these letters will get into your children's hands."

She raised her tear-stained face, taking hope from what he said and the way he said it. "You're sure of that, Inspector?"

"Yes, I'm sure of it."

"But—how can you be?"

"You have ways of watching the mails, don't you, Inspector?" Ben Davidson interposed.

"Yes." Madden had already made up his mind that as a

precaution against a slip-up he would have a cover put on the Davidsons' mail starting tomorrow.

"So you see," Ben said to his wife. "You're borrowing trouble, darling. Haven't we got enough as it is?"

She gave him an uncertain smile. "I'm sorry. It's just that when I think of the children I get sick. I can stand anything for us but not for them."

"Yes, I know," her husband said. He walked back and forth across the room, turned to Madden, and said bitterly, "If someone's got a knife out for me, why bring the children into it? Wouldn't you think it would be enough, doing me out of a promotion at the bank?"

"Has that happened?"

"Yes, it has. I'm supposed to be cleared, Hasbrouck told me he realized I was the fall guy in the Newton affair, but still—I could tell from the way he spoke that no promotion will be coming my way. He's fair enough himself, but I've become a tainted character as far as Jenner's concerned."

"He won't be chairman of the board forever," Madden reminded him.

"He will be long enough to make sure no promotion comes my way," Ben Davidson stated flatly.

It was his wife's turn to offer comfort, his plight distracting her from her worries about the children. She told him he couldn't be sure yet he wouldn't get the promotion, that he was the one who was borrowing trouble now.

When they were calmer, Madden, not satisfied that his vacation resort theory would ever be substantiated, and regarding the point of contact between Newton and Fairmount as a major issue in the case, was ready to question them on it again. He had questioned them separately before, now he questioned them together, hoping that by jogging each other's memories they might recall some new fact relating to it. But they could think of

172

none. When he left them he had no more information on it than when he arrived.

He didn't like tonight's developments. Nothing had been learned from the Davidsons and the letters tended to get more vicious all the time with the threat to send one to the Davidson children just about the worst of all.

His thoughts fidgeted and circled around his next step on the way home and long after he was in bed, disconnected thoughts that settled nowhere. . . .

Inez Blaine, smooth surface and bitchy depths—she'd never confess, he'd have to prove his case against her to the hilt. . . . Two mailings to the pharmacy box, only two, not much to set up a watch on, not much to justify asking Bill Palmisano to put aside an important case of his own in order to start keeping it . . . not much. . . .

Typewriter salesman, try that? No, let it alone. . . . For how long with the letters getting worse all the time? . . . Long enough to prove beyond all doubt that she was writing them before he let it alone that long? . . .

Three already this week and it was only Wednesday. Building into something or just a smart-alecky defiance of him?

Two mailings in the pharmacy box, only two. . . . Should he, shouldn't he ask Bill to start keeping a watch right away? . . .

At long last, Madden, dropping off to sleep, decided to wait and see, wait through tomorrow at least.

Mr. Hasbrouck phoned him the next morning and said that his secretary had collected several more typing samples from typewriters owned by bank people.

"That's fine," said Madden, asking himself if Mr. Hasbrouck shouldn't get special mention in his final report on the case for co-operation given. No, he reflected with a grin, Mr. Hasbrouck's motives weren't pure enough, weren't guided by selfless dictates of public service. Mr. Hasbrouck, understandably, had just one aim in the whole affair; he wanted the bank taken off the hook and Mr. Jenner out of his hair.

At the moment Madden was studying the samples given him Monday, comparing them with Mrs. Davidson's letter. Three of them were so patently dissimilar that he saw no need to send them to Washington. The others, K documents 17, 18, 19 he would send with the letter, the latest Q document.

He said, "Would you mind putting them in the mail for me, Mr. Hasbrouck? I'm pretty busy and I don't know what time I'll be able to get out there today."

"All right, I'll get them off right away." Mr. Hasbrouck's pause brought in another voice from the background. Then he said, "Mr. Jenner's here. He was hoping you'd be out this morning and he'd have a chance to talk with you."

"I'm afraid not," the inspector replied. "Things have been piling up on me a bit here."

"Is there anything new on the case?"

Madden thought he detected a hard-pressed note in the bank president's voice. He said, "We're working on it pretty steadily, Mr. Hasbrouck. My aide is out right now trying to trace the typewriter. But it takes time. Everything we're doing takes time."

"Yes, I guess it does." The words sagged. Clearly, Mr. Hasbrouck was finding it no picnic to cope with Jenner, but there was nothing Madden could do about it except to say he would keep in touch, that he hoped there would be a break in the case soon. He hung up and was heartless enough to find entertainment in the picture he conjured up of Mr. Hasbrouck trying to find enough meat in what he had said to placate the chairman of the board.

Madden spent most of the day with an assistant United States Attorney going over details of a case that was nearly ready to come up for trial. He got back to his office just ahead of his aide, who came in to report that he had

174

now covered all the typewriter agencies with barren results.

When he left, Madden filled in his daily report for the inspector in charge in Boston, and was preparing to leave when Rod phoned to tell him another letter had been mailed, this one addressed to Mr. Hasbrouck. "It was in the same box," he added. "We cleared it first today."

"Well, very active week, isn't it?" Madden commented. "Most active we've had so far. I'll come out after dinner and meet you at the post office. Will you find out if Hasbrouck's going to be home so that I can deliver the letter to him? If he isn't, let me know."

When Rod didn't call back, the postal inspector started for Fairmount soon after seven, puzzling over the sudden rash of letters. Did it mean Mrs. Blaine had seized on chance access to the typewriter for a real fling, or was she creating opportunities to use it for the purpose of ridiculing him?

He didn't know. He did know that he would set up a watch on the pharmacy box tomorrow.

It was Thursday night. Mr. Hasbrouck would ordinarily have been at the bank until nine but had come home early to see the inspector.

He answered the door himself when the inspector arrived and took him into the library. Reading his letter, he exclaimed aloud and shook his head.

"Good God," he said as he handed it back to Madden. "I've never read anything like this in my life. It's a terrible letter. The others were mild by comparison."

Madden read it and agreed with the bank president. It was a terrible letter, violent and profane in its jibes at Mr. Hasbrouck for keeping Lucia in her job, seething with ugliness in its interpretation of her friendship with Rod Harrison, the only man named in it.

"Good God," Mr. Hasbrouck said again. "It's enough

175

to give you the creeps." He stood up, walked across the room and went back to his chair. "I feel as if the whole thing is getting ready to explode in our faces, Inspector. As for Lucia—I don't know, I don't know. Claude—Mr. Jenner—said that if we had just one more letter about her we'd act on her resignation. Just one more—and here it is."

The bank president was on his feet again, unable to sit still, moving to the fireplace to stare into its emptiness. "Perhaps for her own protection she should go home to her mother," he said over his shoulder. "A leave of absence?" He was talking to himself now. "Claude would probably go along with that."

He turned to face Madden. "I really don't want to let her go. She's done so well at the bank and she's a very nice girl too. It's not right for her to lose her job over this. She really needs it since her father died. She doesn't say much about it, but I know her mother's financial position isn't too good nowadays and that Lucia helps her all she can. But even if her salary didn't mean so much, it still wouldn't be right for her to lose her job over something that's not her doing at all."

"Well then, don't let her lose it." Madden's tone was matter-of-fact. "Why tell Mr. Jenner the letter came? I'll take it away with me and as far as you're concerned that's the end of it."

Mr. Hasbrouck made a startled sound in his throat. Madden went on, "I'm hoping to get somewhere with this case within the next few days. After holding out this long it would be too bad, wouldn't it, to let Lucia Ruyter go when it's nearly over?"

Mr. Hasbrouck swallowed audibly. Madden wanted to laugh. This was mutiny, a conspiracy to keep Jenner uninformed, a thing inconceivable to the conscientious bank president.

But the latter, after the first shock of it, paid tribute to

Lucia as an employee or perhaps it was to the cause of fairness, and said he wouldn't mention the letter to Mr. Jenner, who, Madden suspected, would be less ready to fire Lucia himself if her father were still alive, instead, recognizing some sort of class obligation to a fellow-banker.

Madden took the letter away with him and had his laugh after he was out of the house. The bank president had crossed a gulf tonight in conniving to keep things from Jenner. The next time he felt moved to do it, it would come more easily to him. And thus the downward path, reflected Madden. Or, in this case, the upward one?

It was satisfying to picture the board chairman having more and more things kept from him until at last he knew so little about bank affairs that he was reduced to a figurehead.

Jenner a figurehead? This was fantasy, Madden told himself cheerfully. But pleasant, very pleasant. . . .

When he reached the outskirts of Dunston, he turned off into a residential section. It wasn't too late, he thought, to drop in on Ann Lanier if she was home and there were no cars out in front to indicate visitors. She would give him a drink and an hour or two of conversation that would have nothing to do with his case. If he couldn't see her, he'd go along home and catch up on stamp news in Linn's.

But Ann Lanier was home, had no other visitors, and, as always, welcomed him eagerly. Too eagerly, perhaps.

Chapter Sixteen

Lucia felt good the next morning. Rod had been waiting for her the night before when she'd left the bank at nine o'clock. They'd had coffee, gone for a drive and back to her apartment where they'd talked until nearly midnight. He had kidded her about being limited to dates with him at the moment. But when he'd kissed her goodnight he'd said that was the way he'd like it to be from now on.

She walked to the bank instead of taking her car that morning, enjoying the sharpness of the air as she drew it deep into her lungs, the dazzling sky, the bright sun that promised spring was only weeks away, that any day might bring a foretaste of it.

She laughed at herself going up the steps to the bank. I'm falling in love, she thought, and having all the standard reactions.

Mr. Hasbrouck didn't, of course, mention his most recent letter to her, and Lucia's lightheartedness persisted all day. She left the bank at three to drive to Lowell where her mother was giving a party that night to celebrate her grandmother Ruyter's seventieth birthday. Rod phoned while she was packing the few essentials she'd take home with her, told her to have a good trip and that he'd see her Sunday when she got back. Lucia felt

179

even more lighthearted as she set out for Lowell.

That same day Madden found in his morning mail an air-mail letter from Pittsburgh. His colleague there, he reflected with satisfaction, had been wonderfully prompt in responding to the note of urgency in his last letter.

His satisfaction turned into triumph as he read the letter with its list of eleven Newton people who'd had mail forwarded to them at vacation resorts last summer. There on the list was Mrs. Arthur Chapin, Bar Harbor, Maine, July–August.

He picked up the phone and put in a call to the Pittsburgh inspector. But here he ran into a snag. The Pittsburgh office said the inspector was out of town and wouldn't be available until Monday.

Madden hung up, but his hand still hovered over the phone. Call Mrs. Chapin himself? "Did you meet Mrs. Blaine from Fairmount, Connecticut, at Bar Harbor last summer and tell her about Ben Davidson's arrest in Newton in 1934?" It wouldn't do. He knew nothing about Mrs. Chapin or how friendly she'd become with Inez Blaine. It would have to be handled through the Pittsburg inspector.

He rang for the stenographer and dictated an air-mail letter to his colleague, requesting him to see Mrs. Chapin at the earliest possible moment.

By the time the letter was dictated, Inspector Palmisano, free for their scheduled conference, appeared in Madden's office shaking his head.

"What a jerk I just got rid of," he said, dropping down in a chair beside Madden's desk. "Seems he got engaged to this woman out in Omaha through a pen pal club and for two years he's been sending her money, close to three thousand altogether, while she's been stalling him along on when they'd get married. So now it turns out that she's married already and was playing him for all she could get. But this guy won't sign a complaint, doesn't want action taken against her. You figure it out. He's been had for three thousand."

"Pride," Madden commented. "Doesn't want anyone to find out about it."

"Yeah," Palmisano agreed. "I should live to see the day when I'd put my pride ahead of three thousand bucks." He slid lower in the chair and inquired, "Well, what's new in your poison pen case?"

Madden outlined the latest developments and went on to the watch he wanted the younger man to keep on the pharmacy box. "I'd like to get it started today," he said. "Only two letters have been mailed on Friday so far, but this has been such an active week that there might be one." He paused before he added, "I haven't got a picture of Mrs. Blaine to give you. I guess you'll just have to get a picture of everyone who mails a letter. You might as well to be on the safe side."

Palmisano, as blond as a Nordic in spite of his Italian blood, raised a blond eyebrow. "No chance of getting Mrs. Blaine's right away?"

"No, not right away. I've had Johnny on the phone all morning calling the newspapers and every photographer in Dunston. It's no dice, though, around here. There are a couple of photographers in Fairmount, but I don't dare go near them or the Fairmount newspaper where they must have her picture on file. I'm afraid it might get back to her. That's the hell of these smaller towns; you never know who knows who."

Palmisano nodded. "All right, what does she look like?"

"Middle-aged, dark eyes, dark hair cut quite short, well dressed, trim figure, about five-five, weighs maybe a hundred and thirty-five or so."

"A lot of women will answer that description."

"I know. One thing more. If she sees anyone she knows, she has a smile you can't miss. Lady of the manor greeting the tenantry."

"Oh, that type," said Palmisano. Then he said, "I hope we can nail her mailing a letter."

Madden gave him a lazy smile. "Bulldog for facts, aren't you? I'm pretty sure I can lay my hands on the typewriter but I haven't risked a move toward it yet. My Bar Harbor contact still has to be verified, and all I've heard from Seattle is that Gibb Blaine's letter has been delivered to him and the operation set up to get it back. I have to exercise patience and wait for facts."

"These psychos who write letters," Palmisano said. "You could go nuts yourself trying to figure them out."

"Mrs. Blaine's a complicated one if that's what she is. A bully, a snob, a sadist—" Madden broke off with a laugh. "Character analysis done while you wait."

"She sounds like a pip," Palmisano said.

Their conversation turned to details of setting up the watch on the pharmacy box. When these were settled Palmisano returned to his office and Madden, a little later, headed for Fairmount.

Before he went to the post office he stopped across the street from the pharmacy box to make a final survey of the terrain.

He found Rod in his office and sat down with him to discuss the plans he had made. Rod had never played a part in such an arrangement before, so Madden took pains in going over it with him step by step; where Palmisano would park his car, which carrier would clear the box, the signal he would use if he found one of the letters, the least conspicuous method of getting him back and forth.

Madden left the post office well before the time Palmisano was due to arrive there. They would take care not to be seen together in Fairmount.

Chapter Seventeen

At two o'clock Inspector Palmisano entered the Fairmount post office. He was new in the territory, and none of the clerks recognized him as he crossed the lobby to the postmaster's office. Rod was waiting to tell him that the details Madden had left in his hands had been taken care of, including the preempting of parking space directly across the street from the pharmacy box by Rod's car.

"The box faces in toward the sidewalk," Rod explained to Palmisano. "Everyone who uses it will be facing your way, and you'll have a clear view of them because there's a hydrant a couple of feet away that will keep cars from parking close enough to block the box off from you."

They went outside. From the front steps of the post office they could see the pharmacy a few doors away and the collection box at the edge of the sidewalk.

Rod walked up the street to his car and started the motor. When he saw Palmisano's car approaching he pulled out and Palmisano drove in. A sign nearby said that this was a sixty-minute parking zone, but Rod had made a phone call to the police that eliminated the possibility of Palmisano's having to produce his identification at an awkward moment.

He had a newspaper and a magazine on the seat beside him. After a glance across the street he shifted the angle of his rearview mirror to bring the box into his range of vision. His next action was to take a small movie camera out of the glove compartment and lay it on the seat beside him covered by the magazine. Then he picked up the newspaper and appeared to become absorbed in it, paying no attention when the pharmacy box was cleared routinely by a carrier returning to the post office.

It was the quietest period of the afternoon. The high school crowd hadn't yet come downtown from school, the morning rush of Friday shoppers was over, the afternoon rush that would build up to an early evening peak hadn't begun. Only fifteen people, five men, nine women, none of them resembled the description Madden had given of Mrs. Blaine, and a boy, dropped mail into the box in the half-hour between two-thirty and three. All had their pictures taken by Palmisano, the camera camouflaged by the newspaper.

The rest of the time, with the newspaper propped against the steering wheel, Palmisano looked to passers-by like a man waiting for someone. Now and then he sent a bored glance to his watch and yawned.

At three o'clock a mail truck drew into the curb across the street a few feet from the box, a carrier got out, unlocked it, and removed the mail. Palmisano took his picture and immediately thereafter swung the camera to a clock in the pharmacy window to mark a half-hour of film footage. Then, in the rear-view mirror, he watched the carrier go through the mail looking for one of the letters under the guise of arranging it face up. While he was facing it, a woman approached him, smiled, said something, and handed him a letter to add to the collection. Palmisano took her picture too, regardless of the improbability of anyone handing a poison pen letter to a carrier.

The woman walked away out of sight while Palmisano watched for the prearranged signal, the carrier taking off his cap and wiping his forehead with his handkerchief if he found one of the letters.

The signal didn't come. He finished facing the mail, put it in his bag, went to the truck and drove away.

No letter in that batch.

Between three and three-thirty, business picked up at the box, more than doubled, in fact, while the camera hummed recording it.

At three-thirty the mail truck drove up again, the same carrier emptied the box and, as before, took his time facing the mail.

Palmisano took his picture, then the clock in the pharmacy window and waited for the signal.

It didn't come. The carrier put the mail in his bag and went away. At four o'clock, at four-thirty, there was still no signal. By that time the street was thronged with an ever-increasing flow of people, going in and out of the stores, hurrying along the sidewalks, mailing letters, more and more of them stopping at the box to drop them in.

Men and women of all ages and sizes, an occasional child, Palmisano went on taking their pictures, giving his closest attention to women who bore a resemblance to Inez Blaine.

There were moments when his pretense of indolent waiting wore very thin, so busy was his camera. But no one seemed to be watching him closely. It was mostly girls who gave him a second glance as they went by, their attention caught by the fact that Palmisano was a good-looking young man, a stranger they might like to know. The patrolman on the beat took care not to notice him during the earlier part of the afternoon, and from four o'clock on spent most of his time breaking up traffic jams.

Not long after the four-thirty clearing of the box a woman approached it, middle-aged, with dark eyes and hair, a figure still trim as far as Palmisano could tell from the loose topcoat she wore. He took another look as he focused the camera for a shot of her dropping a piece of mail into the box. She might be Mrs. Blaine, he thought, with quickened interest. She seemed preoccupied, looking at no one, speaking to no one as she turned and walked away.

At five o'clock while the carrier was facing the mail he took off his cap and wiped his forehead with his handkerchief.

Palmisano was ahead of him getting back to the post office.

The letter the carrier turned over to him was addressed to Lucia. Palmisano showed it to Rod, who said, "I don't think you'll be able to deliver it to her, Inspector. She's going home for the week end and must have left over an hour ago." He picked up the phone. "I'll try her number, though, just to make sure."

He dialed Lucia's number but there was no answer. She was on her way to Lowell. The letter couldn't be held up, it would have to reach her by mail.

Palmisano called Madden to report it, and a few minutes later went back to Dunston where he left the roll of film with a photographer who could be relied on to give them overnight service in developing it, and then went on to the Federal Building to fill Madden in on the details of his afternoon.

The latter was waiting for him in his office. He had regarded Palmisano's watch today as something of a dry run, feeling that it was almost too much to hope that with several letters already sent this week another one would be mailed today. Monday had figured so consistently in the pattern that this was the day on which he expected the watch to bear fruit. In preparation for it, he had sent

186

his aide to Fairmount that afternoon with instructions to station himself with his polaroid camera as close as he could get to the Blaines' to try for pictures of Mrs. Blaine going in or out of her house.

As he waited for Palmisano, he considered keeping a watch tomorrow and decided against it. There could be no definite hours set for it; no Saturday mailings had taken place so far. It would have to be an all-day watch, and even with another inspector to relieve Palmisano they'd be bound to attract some attention sitting in a car opposite the pharmacy box for hours on end. If a room with a window overlooking it had been available, there would be no problem. But there was none, surveillance had to be maintained from a car. He'd let Saturday go and wait for Monday.

His aide phoned him at home that night to report that he'd been able to get two pictures of Inez but that neither one was good enough for identification purposes. Madden told him not to try again tomorrow; they'd wait to see what they had on the film.

The aide's pictures of Inez had been taken as she got out of her car in the driveway and hurried into the house, late getting home and planning to go out to a committee meeting after dinner.

This was one of her bad days. There were many of them lately, days when loneliness overcame her and loathing of the whole world.

At breakfast she looked at Alec with icy contempt. She could scarcely stand the sight of him since the letters had made him more humble than ever in his efforts to please her.

"Get your lunch downtown today," she told him curtly. "I won't be here."

He didn't ask where she'd be. He said, "All right, dear,

187

have a nice day."

She didn't answer him. After he left she drove to Dunston on an extravagant shopping spree that Alec wouldn't dare reproach her for when the bills came in, lunched at an expensive restaurant, and stopped for cocktails at an expensive bar on the way home. But the cocktails didn't raise her spirits. Her mood was even more sullen and bitter than before.

It was late afternoon by that time. The rest of the way to Fairmount she brooded over Lucia. She'd written violent things about her yesterday in a letter to Dick Hasbrouck, but would it do any good? Would another letter to Jenner do any good?

She pounded the wheel in frustration. "The goddamned fools keeping a tramp like her at the bank!"

Inez had begun to believe that what she wrote about Lucia was true.

She didn't feel like going straight home when she reached Fairmount and instead went to the Visiting Nurse office. No one was there. She sat down at the Smith Corona, her fingers flying over the keys in a letter to Lucia filled with savage, obscene threats of what was going to happen to her pretty soon.

She addressed an envelope, put the letter in it, and ran the flap over a wet sponge she kept in the desk. When it was sealed and stamped she felt better for the moment, secure in a sense of power she could exercise at will. Just wait till Lucia got this letter, she gloated to herself. It would scare her stiff.

But by the time she mailed it downstown her mood, like a pendulum, had swung back to bitter discontent. She went home.

Sunday at dinner Alec said, "Mrs. Cummings wants me to bring in a two-page sample from our typewriter tomorrow, Inez."

Her heart leaped with fear. "What for? What's our

188

typewriter got to do with it?"

"Well, they're asking everyone." He told her about Madden's request for samples.

She quieted as she listened. As long as the thing was general it was all right.

But as Alec went on talking about typewriter identification, relaying what he'd heard at the bank, Inez became frightened again. She hadn't realized that each individual machine could be identified, she'd thought of it only in terms of the make and perhaps the model.

Later on, alone in the kitchen stacking the dishes in the dishwasher, her mind teemed with thoughts of the typewriter and Madden. Gone was her feeling of being out of his reach. She couldn't convince herself that she was perfectly safe, that there was no earthly reason for him to check on typewriters at the VNA. She was too frightened.

Then, putting food away in the refrigerator, she leaned against it suddenly limp with relief. She'd thought of a way to protect herself. She'd buy a secondhand portable from the Smith Corona dealer in Dunston and substitute it for the one at the agency. The one that was there she'd take home and keep hidden in the attic.

She'd go to Dunston tomorrow. No, she couldn't. She was due at the Well Child Conference at nine in the morning, and her whole day would be taken up with it. But Tuesday she'd get the typewriter and after that Inspector Madden could do all the checking he pleased at the VNA. Actually, of course, he wouldn't go near the place, there was no earthly reason why he should. But, still, she'd get the typewriter.

Saturday afternoon Madden set up a movie projector in his office facing a blank wall that would serve as a screen, inserted the film he and Palmisano had picked

189

up at the photographer's, and started the machine. A procession of people began to pass before them on the wall. A man appeared first, shuffling along, bent and shaky with age. He dropped a piece of mail in the box, paused to take out his handkerchief, and blow his nose and moved away. Then came a woman with a crying child trailing after her. She pulled down the lid of the box, not watching as she dropped in several pieces of mail, looking at the child, her face distorted with anger, her lips moving rapidly.

"I could hear her yelling at the kid clear across the street," Palmisano said.

Two girls giggling and clutching at each other came next. A businessman followed, then a young mother wheeling a baby. A man in overalls and a plaid jacket came next. The mail truck appeared, the carrier cleared the box, Palmisano's shot of the clock in the pharmacy window showed that it was four-thirty. The truck drove away, a woman, a man, another woman put mail into the box.

Palmisano sat up straighter. "You'll see the one I thought might be Mrs. Blaine any minute," he said.

But an ancient crone with bird's-nest hair came next and then a boy, sloppy, grimy-looking to the camera's eye.

"No shining morning face there," Madden commented.

"Didn't have to have one, it was afternoon," Palmisano said.

"Don't be so literal-minded when—" Madden cut himself short as Inez Blaine came within the camera's range, walked up to the box, dropped in a piece of mail, and walked away.

"That her?" Palmisano asked.

"Yes," said Madden while the film continued to unwind revealing a procession of people unknown to

190

him. Then the mail truck appeared again, the carrier facing the mail, giving the signal that he'd found one of the letters.

Madden shut off the projector and said with deep satisfaction, "She's it, all right."

"She sure is."

"Monday should be our day to nab her. So far she hasn't missed mailing a letter on Monday. Now that you know who she is, we'll get a key to the box for you."

"Let's just hope she doesn't mail anything else along with a poison pen," Palmisano remarked.

"Yes," said Madden, "let's hope so. If she doesn't," he went on grimly, "I look forward to going to her with her letter and a list of everything else you find in the box and asking her to give me a description of what she mailed."

"Let's go have a drink on it," Palmisano said.

"Okay." Madden grinned. "Nothing like having a drink to chickens that haven't hatched yet."

At two-thirty Monday afternoon Palmisano took up his watch again. Today he had a key to the box and knew who he was watching for. If Mrs. Blaine used it, he would open it as soon as she was gone, take out and list every piece of mail in it. A poison pen letter would at once be turned over to Madden. The rest of the mail would be put in covering envelopes with a note enclosed to the postmaster in the town of its destination, asking that it be delivered personally to the addressee. The addressee would then be requested to turn it back to the post office or sign a deposition describing what it was and the date and circumstances of its delivery.

Palmisano, behind his newspaper, was alert to everyone who came or went along the street. Unlike Friday, it was quiet in the downtown section the whole afternoon. He missed no one, he felt certain, who mailed a letter, least of all Mrs. Blaine. But she did not appear, and no signal came from the carrier who cleared the box

191

every half-hour.

For all his casual manner, Palmisano was a conscientious young man and he grew more and more worried as the afternoon drew to a close. She had been mailing the letters every Monday since they started until today. Had he somehow given the game away, frightened her off on her way to the box?

He didn't see how this could have happened but still he worried about it.

Soon after six o'clock Rod Harrison drove past and with a nod toward the post office indicated that Palmisano was to give up his vigil and go back there.

David Madden, who had been keeping a vigil of his own at the post office since three o'clock, was in the postmaster's office with Rod when Palmisano arrived. The post office had closed for the day, and except for a working crew dispatching the night collection the building was empty.

Palmisano sat down and looked at the other two. "Did a letter get mailed in a different box?" he asked.

"No," Madden replied, his narrow dark brows drawn in thought. "The first Monday she's missed. The question is, has my investigation finally scared her off or is there another explanation such as going away for the day or entertaining company or something of that sort?"

He fell silent and then said, "I suppose I could ask Lucia to try and find out from Blaine tomorrow what went on at their house today. I have to see her anyway to pick up Friday's letter." He added to Palmisano, "Rod says she hasn't opened it and doesn't intend to open any more of them."

"She'll be home tonight," Rod contributed. "I told her you were going to be out here today and would probably drop by to pick up the letter. As a matter of fact, I told her I'd drop by myself tonight."

Madden eyed him quizzically. "You saw her last night

192

too when she got back from her trip up home." He turned to Pamisano and remarked solemnly, "A loyal employee of the POD. Since the young lady has limited her dating on account of the letters, Rod had stepped into the breach. Quite nobly, too, I would say, living up to the highest traditions of the Service."

Rod, bright red, joined in their laughter.

"I bet she's a doll," Palmisano said.

"She is," Rod agreed fervently.

"Yes indeed," Madden chimed in. "I haven't figured out yet just how Rod got in ahead of me so fast."

A moment later the light note was gone from his voice as he said to the young inspector, "We'll try it again tomorrow."

"Another day, another car, and, I think, another newspaper," said Palmisano. "People must be getting tired of the *Times*, I'll change to the *Tribune*."

He stood up, yawned, and stretched. "Well, I'll go along now if you don't need me any more tonight, Dave."

"No, you run along. And thanks very much."

"See you tomorrow." He sent Rod a grin. "Hold the fort now with Miss Ruyter."

"I'll try." Rod grinned back at him.

Palmisano left, Madden suggested to Rod that it was time he went home to dinner.

"What about you?" Rod asked.

"Oh, I'll have something at a restaurant and then go over to Lucia's. I'll see you there, won't I?"

Rod looked hesitant. "Well, if you want to have a talk with her alone—"

"You join us," Madden said, "and we'll pool our ideas. You have some pretty good ones, you know."

"I'll be there." The younger man looked pleased over the compliment that came from a source he valued highly.

They went out to their cars and separated. Rod drove

out of the parking lot first, Madden lingered to light a cigarette and turn a reflective glance on the building in front of him, one of so many around which a large part of his life revolved.

Lights still burned in the workroom where, under the clerk in charge, the last mail of the day was being dispatched. Now and then Madden liked to let his fancy roam among the letters in it, the good news and the bad being started on its way to many people in many places.

It was pleasanter to think of the good news: Jim got his promotion today and we're so thrilled and happy. . . . I can't wait for you to see the baby, just this week he's gained two pounds. . . . Yes, I'd love to come, I know we'll have a wonderful time. . . . The enclosed check is to wish you a happy birthday with all our love. . . .

Then there were the others: She's to go to the hospital tomorrow but they're not sure her heart will stand an operation. . . . If we don't have your check in the mail within the next five days we will be forced to institute legal action. . . . I'm terribly sorry, I didn't mean to fall in love with him but you've been away for such a long time now. . . .

It was all there, good news and bad being sorted with swift, impersonal competence. . . .

Chapter Eighteen

While the postal inspector was having dinner at a Fairmount restaurant, Rod, having finished his, was in his room trying to decide which of three ties looked best with the gray shirt he had just put on, and Lucia was serving tea and toast to Mrs. Aitken.

She had gone in to see her landlady after dinner and found her on a sofa in the living room nursing a head cold. No, she said, she'd had no dinner and didn't want any. But Lucia had insisted on tea and toast and fixed a tray for her.

"You're so kind," Mrs. Aitken said gratefully. Then, as she sat up to let Lucia plump up the pillows in back of her, she moaned, "Just look at me! Nose like a tomato, eyes all red. It's simply maddening to come down with a cold right now when I have to go to a BMO—Board Members Organization—meeting in Dunston tomorrow."

"You'll have to skip it, that's all," Lucia said.

"I can't. I have to go if it kills me. It's a state level thing, and as president of the VNA board I'm to present a report on six months' findings in long-term illnesses—chronics, that is."

"Can't someone else do it for you?"

Mrs. Aitken sipped tea, shook her head. "I have to do

it myself.''

"What awful luck," Lucia sympathized. "But perhaps you'll feel a little better tomorrow. The first day's always the worst with a cold, I think. Look, why don't I turn down your bed and as soon as you've finished your tea and toast you crawl in and get a good night's sleep. It might make all the difference in the world in how you feel tomorrow."

"I can't go to bed yet." An exasperated note sounded in the older woman's hoarse voice. "I'm waiting up for the report to be brought to me. Mrs. Burdett called awhile ago all apologies that it wasn't ready yet. There were some last-minute figures she had to check, and then it seems there was some misunderstanding about which of the volunteers was to type it. The whole thing sounded like such a mix-up I didn't even attempt to follow it. Anyway, the report was to be brought over to me by half past six, seven o'clock at the latest, and here it is nearly half past seven now and not a sign of it. It's just too much on top of this cold." Mrs. Aitken sank back against the pillows as she spoke and pressed a fresh wad of tissues against her nose.

"I could call the nurse for you," Lucia suggested. "But she's not apt to be there at this hour, is she?"

"No, it wouldn't do a bit of good to call," Mrs. Aitken fretted. "You'd only get whoever's typing it and she'd tell you she'd bring it right over, and then when it didn't get here I'd be twice as upset as I am now."

"Well then, why don't I just run over there and see what's holding up the works?"

"Oh, but you've put your car in the garage and it would be a nuisance for you to go out back and get it out again tonight." Mrs. Aitken looked at her hopefully as she made this protest.

"I won't even bother with my car," Lucia said. "The VNA is just around the corner on Arch Street, isn't it?"

"Well, it's a little walk—the old gray house, you know, that used to be the Thompson place. But I really mustn't put you to so much trouble."

"No trouble at all." Lucia was already on her feet. "Much more satisfactory to go than to phone if we're dealing with a volunteer who isn't reliable. I need toothpaste anyway, so I'll go to the drugstore while I'm out. And I'll come back with the report. Snatch it out of the volunteer's hands, if I must."

At the door she turned to say, "Oh, Rod Harrison's coming. If he gets here before I'm back, will you let him in my place and tell him I'll be right along?"

"Yes, I'll tell him."

Lucia left from her own apartment a few minutes later. The VNA building wasn't quite as near as she had made it sound. Just around the corner was actually two long blocks to Arch Street and then another long block on Arch Street itself.

But the night was clear, not too cold, the air just crisp enough to keep Lucia moving at a good pace under the leafless trees, looking up now and then at the stars, pinpoints of light in the moonless sky, or into lighted houses along the way. An occasional car passed her, but she met no other pedestrians.

Arch Street was darker when she turned onto it with patches of snow, left over from last week's light fall, more noticeable here than on the street she had just left. The first few houses she passed were imposing structures set far back from the street in spacious grounds. Most of them were in darkness with their owners, older moneyed people, in Florida for the winter. The last in the row, surrounded by a high, impenetrable hedge and with a chain hooked across the driveway between stone gateposts, belonged, Lucia knew, to the Bradfords. Just last year, Mr. Bradford, now in his eighties, had given up his directorship at the bank.

197

As she glanced at the house, its pillars gleaming white in the distance among the masses of shrubbery that filled the grounds, her step quickened involuntarily. It seemed to her that there was something eerie about it standing dark and deserted midway between two widely spaced street lights.

Beyond it the island of wealth ended, the houses, closer together and nearer the sidewalk, became less imposing, although still substantial with none of them crowding its neighbors. The Visiting Nurse building, once a private home, stood almost at the end of the block, deeply shadowed by tall old trees on its grounds. Its upper floor, where the Chamber of Commerce had rooms, was in darkness, but lights shone in the hall and one of the rooms downstairs and a car stood in the parking area in back. The volunteer must still be working on Mrs. Aitken's report, Lucia thought. She might as well go the drugstore first and then stop for the report.

She went around the corner to a neighborhood drugstore, one of several small businesses that had spread out into the area, bought toothpaste, and went back to the agency.

Inez Blaine answered the door when she rang the bell. They exchanged startled glances. Lucia said, "Why, Mrs. Blaine—" and then, "Good evening."

"Good evening." Inez' tone was flat, her usual graciousness not in evidence.

They had seen each other at the bank now and then, but this was the first time they'd met face to face since Gibb had gone to Seattle. Inez, caught unawares, couldn't conceal her hostility.

Lucia was taken aback by it but knew right away what the reason for it must be. Mrs. Blaine resented the fact that she'd turned Gibb down. It was nonsense, of course, for her to believe this had been a great blow to her self-centered son. Apparently she did believe it, though, and until this moment Lucia hadn't realized how she felt.

Inez waited for her to explain her presence. Lucia said, "I've come for a report Mrs. Aitken has to give at a meeting tomorrow, Mrs. Blaine. Some volunteer is supposed to be typing it for her."

"Well . . ." The older woman hesitated so long that it seemed as if she didn't intend to go on. At last she said, "The volunteer had to leave before it was done. Mrs. Burdett asked me to finish it."

"Oh. I knew you were on the VNA board but I didn't realize—" Lucia broke off, eying her in perplexity, wondering why her reluctance to speak somehow stood apart from the hostility she displayed instead of growing out of it.

"We board members do all sorts of things here." Inez Blaine's tone left no room for questions about her own role at the agency. She added, "You can tell Mrs. Aitken that the report is nearly finished and I'll drop it off in a few minutes on my way home."

Lucia started to say, "All right," and didn't. Inez' manner, the unwelcoming way she stood, blocking off the doorway as if to deny admittance, aroused in the girl a sudden resolve not to accept this summary dismissal. She said politely but firmly, "I'll wait for it, Mrs. Blaine, since it's nearly finished. I told Mrs. Aitken I'd bring it back with me. She's quite disturbed that she doesn't have it yet."

"She won't be as soon as she hears I'm working on it," Inez said with cold firmness of her own.

"I promised her, though, that I'd bring it back with me, so I think I'd better wait for it." Lucia stepped forward as she spoke.

Short of slamming the door in her face and having her go back to Mrs. Aitken to report what extraordinary treatment she'd received, there was little the older woman could do.

199

For a moment, from her expression, it seemed that she would slam the door in Lucia's face. Instead, she stepped back, allowing her to cross the threshold.

The girl closed the door behind her and found herself in a hall cut in half along its length by a partition that provided a separate entrance to the Chamber of Commerce rooms upstairs. Coming in out of the cold air, she caught the odor of the building, a mingling of the mustiness of age, a medicinal smell, a hint of dampness in the cellar. On her right was a combination office-waiting room, its door held back against the wall by an old flatiron.

Inez led the way into the room. It was furnished with a desk, a standard model typewriter, files, a table that held magazines, a few chairs for clients. An inner door stood open on an unlighted room. Inez closed it. "It creates a draft," she said and went on to the desk. As she seated herself in front of the typewriter she glanced at Lucia, who had halted in the doorway. "If you'll just sit down, this will be finished in a few minutes."

Lucia sat down in the nearest chair. Inez placed a sheet of carbon between two sheets of paper and inserted them in the typewriter. She started to type, copying from notes that lay beside her.

Lucia, presented with a view of her straight back, listening to her sure touch on the keys, thought, "She's a good typist. I didn't even know she could type," and felt a pang of uneasiness without recognizing it for what it was.

She looked at her watch. Quarter of eight. Rod would have arrived before she got home.

For the next few minutes the only sound in the room was the rhythmic clack of the typewriter keys. Lucia counted the sprays of ivy in a tall black glass vase on the desk, took in the fact that Inez seemed to have reached the last page of notes from which she was copying, and should have the report finished very soon.

Twelve minutes of eight. Restlessness, a growing sense of unease that could no longer go unrecognized even though she couldn't account for it, brought Lucia to her feet and over to the magazine table that stood next to the inner door. Like the other door that led into the hall of the old house, it was loose in its frame, perhaps already unlatched from the vibration of the typewriter keys, and needing only the slight extra jar of her footsteps to set it free. Whatever the reason, it swung open just as she reached the table.

Starting to close it, the girl glanced into the room which appeared to be the nurses' private office with a desk for each of them. On one of the desks she saw what at first looked like a small suitcase to her. She looked again, peering into the semi-darkness of the room, and then stood motionless in the doorway. It wasn't a suitcase; it was a portable typewriter case, presumably containing a typewriter. The lid was closed but Lucia knew at once, beyond question or doubt, that the typewriter it contained was a Smith Corona portable.

In the room behind her the clack of the keys ceased, the sudden silence broke in upon her trancelike state. She took a swift step backward, drawing the door shut after her, turned to the table, and scooped up a magazine. Pretending to be absorbed in it, she dared not look around as she heard Inez stand up, walk across the room, and return to the desk. When the typewriter sounded again Lucia, holding her breath, let it out and gathered courage to steal a glance at the older woman, typing steadily again. She hadn't seen her looking in the nurses' office, hadn't stood up from the desk until after Lucia had gotten back to the magazine table.

It seemed safe to return to her chair, her legs weak, her mind in too much of a whirl for her to notice that the hall door had swung out from the wall, no longer held back against it by the heavy old flatiron.

Her one desire was to run out of the building and all the way home to tell Rod about the typewriter. He would know where to locate Inspector Madden—wasn't he in Fairmount anyway?—and with Mrs. Aitken's key the inspector could get in later to take a typing sample from the Smith Corona. Not that he would need it to tell him Mrs. Blaine was writing the letters, Lucia's thoughts continued. She could tell him that herself.

Remembering the obscenities in them, she shivered. Under Mrs. Blaine's mannered surface lay some kind of madness, murky depths that Lucia could never penetrate and wouldn't want to if she could.

If she would just finish the report and let Lucia escape from this nearness to her. It had become a contamination. . . .

Inez, as if in compliance with Lucia's thoughts, glanced around and said, "It will be ready in another minute."

In her wild impatience to get away from there the girl completely missed the tense metallic note in the older woman's voice, although she tried to speak normally herself as she replied, "That's good. I'm in rather a hurry. I have—" She broke off, remembering the things Inez Blaine had written about other dates of hers, and then, her effort at normality shattered, went on hastily, "I have, well, I have quite a lot to do tonight," and stood up to put on her coat.

As Inez took the last page of the report out of the typewriter she turned to look at Lucia, who was shocked by the hatred that flared suddenly in her eyes. A moment later she reached down to open one of the desk drawers. While she was doing this her elbow, seemingly by accident, hit the stacked pages of the report and brushed them off the desk onto the floor.

"Oh," she said, "how clumsy of me."

Lucia's reaction came automatically. She knelt beside

the desk and began to pick up the scattered sheets of paper. Inez rose as if to help her. That was the last thing Lucia remembered; then, explosive pain in the back of her head and oblivion.

Inez Blaine checked her third blow, dismayed by the amount of blood flowing from Lucia's head to form a stain on the linoleum. She dropped the flatiron, ran to the lavatory, and came back with a wad of paper towels. She pressed them into the wounds and rushed back for more to wipe up the blood on the floor. When the last trace of it was removed and the towels disposed of, she bound her own scarf tight around Lucia's head and was satisfied that she had staunched the bleeding.

Looking down at the unconscious girl, she experienced a moment of feeling at peace with herself, the torment of hatred that had obsessed her ever since Lucia's rejection of Gibb drove him away from his home, robbed his mother of the happiness of his daily presence, assuaged at last.

"Serves you right," she said. Then, conscious of the hurrying minutes, she snatched up her coat and put it on.

Her plans were made. She had made them all at once, it seemed, when a flicker of movement, reflected in the black glass vase on the desk, caught her eye and she looked up from her typing and saw Lucia mirrored distortedly in it, standing in the doorway of the nurses' office looking in at the Smith Corona portable, rarely used since the new standard typewriter was bought by the agency last year.

She herself had noticed it earlier on Mrs. Burdett's desk and hadn't liked seeing it out of the closet in plain view. But if the senior nurse was using it, Inez didn't want to connect herself with it by putting it away.

Her thoughts had flown to it the moment Lucia arrived. If only she'd found time to buy a substitute today! She hadn't, though, and here was Lucia Ruyter who had forced her way into the building and, by sneaking around opening doors she had no business to touch, had discovered the portable.

She'd go straight to Inspector Madden about it.

In the first horrified moment, sitting with her hands suspended over the keys, looking at Lucia's reflection in the vase, Inez could think of no way to save herself except to get rid of the portable as soon as Lucia left. But that would be no use, she realized instantly. Reports typed on it were in the files of schools and offices all over town as well as in the VNA's own files; Madden would find them unless she had a substitute portable to throw him off the track.

There was no possible way to get one tonight. Disgrace, imprisonment loomed over her, all the more bitter because they would be brought about by Lucia whom she hated so much.

It was then, all in a rush, that her plan, her salvation, came to her. In the vase she saw Lucia close the door and stood up herself and went across the room to get the flatiron.

Lucia, pretending interest in a magazine, wasn't looking at her as she went back to the desk, put the flatiron in a drawer, sat down, and somehow steadied herself to type, "Gerontologists are agreed that with longevity an increasingly important factor in long-term illnesses. . . ."

Her eye caught a final flicker of movement in the black glass vase as Lucia moved out of its range and returned to her chair, not knowing that she was about to die, that this time she would not escape as she had last November. This time, Inez told herself, as she took the last page of the report out of the typewriter, she had a surer plan. . . .

And now it was in operation.

The next step was to get rid of Lucia. Then she'd put the typewriter in her car to be disposed of for good later on, and deliver the report to Mrs. Aitken, expressing surprise that Lucia was supposed to have picked it up, suggesting that the girl must have stopped to visit someone on her way to the VNA since she hadn't arrived there before Inez left. Mrs. Aitken would fuss a little but she wouldn't do anything about Lucia's absence right away. After all, Lucia was a free agent, Mrs. Aitken only her landlady. She'd think up all kinds of explanations for what was keeping her, it would probably be three or four hours yet before she'd give serious thought to calling the police. Tomorrow, or whenever the police questioned her, Inez would stick to her story that she hadn't seen Lucia tonight.

Tomorrow, the moment Alec left for the bank she'd drive to Dunston, buy a Smith Corona portable, and have it on Mrs. Burdett's desk before one o'clock when the senior nurse would make her first appearance of the day at her office after spending the morning at the psychiatric clinic in Dunston.

As Inez bent over to catch hold of Lucia she hesitated, wondering if she shouldn't take the portable and the report with her now.

No, she thought, she'd go on with the plan she'd mapped out. She'd have to come back anyway with the flatiron, the weapon she'd take with her to use again on Lucia if she needed to. After she'd gotten rid of her she'd feel better prepared to cope with such details as putting the scattered pages of the report together and taking a last careful look around to make sure she'd overlooked nothing that would arouse suspicion tomorrow. The main thing right now was to get Lucia out of there as fast as she could.

She caught hold of the unconscious girl, dragged her out of the room and along the hall to the back door, panting and pulling but not stopping to rest, driven by the need for haste. Getting her down the back steps was easier. Inez left her at the bottom of them while she

205

backed her car up without turning on the lights and then, in the hardest pull of all, got her inside on the floor. After that she ran back into the building for Lucia's pocketbook and the flatiron.

She had picked them up and was ready to leave when the telephone rang. It stopped her dead in the doorway. She had to answer it.

When she lifted the receiver she didn't recognize Mrs. Aitken's voice at first. Then she said, "Oh, it's you, Mrs. Aitken. This is Inez Blaine. Your voice sounds different."

"No wonder," Mrs. Aitken said and told her about her cold. Inez, after forcing herself to listen for a moment or two, broke in on the recital. "By the way, your report's nearly finished. I'll drop it off on my way home."

"Why, that's what I called about. Hasn't Lucia gotten there yet? She left here over half an hour ago to pick it up for me."

"Well, she hasn't arrived yet. Perhaps she stopped somewhere on the way."

"She did say she'd go to the drugstore while she was out," Mrs. Aitken conceded. "But I don't think—"

"Oh, she probably met someone there that she's talking to," Inez interrupted, frantic to put an end to the conversation. "I'm sure she'll be along by the time I've finished the report."

"But you see—"

"I'll hurry up and have it ready for her. Good-by, Mrs. Aitken." Inez dropped the receiver in place, picked up the flatiron and pocketbook, and rushed out of the building, stopping before she got into her car for a glance at Lucia, a motionless bundle on the floor in back. She had the motor started when she thought of the front door. She'd unlocked it to admit Lucia but she couldn't remember locking it again and had to make sure it was locked. With a sound between an oath and a sob she slid out of the car, went into the building by the back door,

206

fumbling in the dark to unlock it, and ran along the hall to the front door. It was locked, the delay had been for nothing.

She was shaking from head to foot. But when she was back in her car she told herself that now the way was paved to maintain for all time to come that she had not seen Lucia tonight.

to give you the creeps." He stood up, walked across the room and went back to his chair. "I feel as if the whole thing is getting ready to explode in our faces, Inspector.

Chapter Nineteen

Not long after Lucia left for the VNA, Mrs. Aitken got up from the sofa and went through the vestibule into Lucia's apartment. Her slight chronic deafness, admitted to no one, was accentuated by her head cold, and she was afraid that from her own part of the house she might not hear Rod Harrison when he arrived.

He rang Lucia's doorbell about fifteen minutes later. Mrs. Aitken admitted him and explained Lucia's absence, adding, "But she'll be back in a few minutes, Rod, if you'll just come in and wait."

Rod followed her into the apartment and sat down. Mrs. Aitken proceeded to tell him about her cold, beginning with the first dry, scratchy feeling in her throat yesterday afternoon and sparing him no detail of its progress since or of the medication she had taken for it.

When Madden arrived she was in the midst of telling Rod about the BMO meeting tomorrow and that she didn't think she would live through it if she felt as bad as she did tonight. Madden joined Rod in sympathizing, but Mrs. Aitken lost interest in her cold for the moment and let her voice die away into silence while she directed puzzled glances at Madden, trying to decide what he was doing at Lucia's when she had a date with Rod.

Was he Rod's rival? If so, they were friendly ones and times had certainly changed since Mrs. Aitken was a girl.

Rod stirred restlessly in his chair, looked at his watch, and remarked, "I wonder what's keeping Lucia." He cocked his head toward the window at the sound of a car outside. "Is that her car now?"

"Oh, didn't I tell you she walked?" Mrs. Aitken said. "Even so, she's had time to get back."

"She walked? Well then—" He broke off to listen again. "I think that's your phone ringing. Perhaps it's Lucia. If it is, will you tell her I'll pick her up?"

"All right, I'll tell her." Mrs. Aitken left, hurrying a little when she reached the vestibule where she herself could hear the phone ringing. But when she reached it, the call wasn't from Lucia, it was from a fellow-member of the garden club, who was prepared to discuss at some length the table centerpiece for a Washington's Birthday dinner. Mrs. Aitken got her off the line as soon as possible and looked at her watch. Ten minutes past eight. Lucia certainly should have been back by this time.

The agency number was familiar to Mrs. Aitken as her own. She dialed it, had her brief, unsatisfactory conversation with Inez cut short by the click of the receiver at the other end just as she started to say, "But you see, Rod Harrison's here and I don't think Lucia can still be at the drugstore when she knew he was coming." She got no farther than, "But you see—" when the click came. She hung up, said "Well!" to herself, and returned to Lucia's apartment.

"That wasn't Lucia," she informed Rod, "so I called the VNA. She hasn't even got there yet. I can't imagine what's keeping her downtown all this time, especially when she was expecting you."

Mrs. Aitken transferred her glance pointedly to

Madden as she spoke to make it clear to him that Rod, a favorite of hers since his boyhood days, had the inside track with Lucia.

"She hasn't even gotten there yet?" Rod said in surprise. "That's funny." He picked up his topcoat and put it on. "I guess I'll take a run downtown and look for her. Do you know which drugstore she was going to, Mrs. Aitken?"

"Try the Fairmount Pharmacy first. That's where she usually goes. I can't imagine, though—"

"I'll try them all. Maybe she's met some guy she likes better." The faint note of concern in Rod's voice didn't match his joking words.

After he left Mrs. Aitken looked at the inspector and said, "I can't help thinking of the time she got hit by a car last fall. But if anything like that happened again, surely by this time—"

Madden was at the front window watching Rod get into his car and head downtown. He turned back to Mrs. Aitken and said, "Are you sure they know what they were talking about at the VNA, Mrs. Aitken? Who answered the phone?"

"Inez Blaine, who's there all alone typing my report. She's on the board, you see, and takes such an interest that she's made herself indispensable. The rest of us are always telling her we don't know how we managed before we had her help."

Madden felt no surprise. From the moment that Mrs. Aitken came back into the room and reported that Lucia hadn't appeared yet at the agency, he had been prepared for what he'd just heard. But he kept his voice matter-of-fact as he said, "I think I'll drive over there while Rod's looking for her downtown. How do I get there, Mrs. Aitken?"

Two blocks to his left from her door, she told him, then

211

turn right, and he'd find the VNA almost at the end of the first block on his right. "There's a sign over the door," she continued. "You can't miss it. But—" She paused. There was no point in reminding Mr. Madden, whoever he was, that he needn't go to the VNA looking for Lucia since Rod would go there himself if he didn't find her downtown. There was no point in it because Madden was already at the door pulling on his topcoat and saying over his shoulder, "Be right back, Mrs. Aitken."

Closing the door after him, he vanished from her ken. If she had been at the front window, Mrs. Aitken would have seen that he was running as he went down the steps and out to his car. But she remained in the chair where she had just seated herself. A little of his sudden tension had reached her, leaving her anxious and confused, aware that something was wrong but not knowing what to do about it.

She looked at the phone. Should she call Inez again and ask if Lucia had gotten there yet?

Better not, she thought. Inez hadn't sounded as if she'd welcome another interruption. Besides, Mr. Madden would be there in his car in another two or three minutes. He'd find Lucia or Rod would find her. There must be some perfectly good explanation for her absence that they'd all overlooked.

Mrs. Aitken gave her sore nose a gingerly pat with tissue, rubbed her heavy head, wished she could go to bed, wished they would come back with Lucia. Something was wrong.

David Madden counted off the two long blocks to Arch Street, turned right on it, and found himself on the longest block of all with big houses on either side, the street deserted, no other car in sight. He slowed down looking at each house on his right, one with the driveway blocked off by a chain hung between stone gateposts,

212

small drifts of snow blown against them, the house itself a dark mass far back from the street.

As he glanced at it his lights picked up a light car coming out of a driveway a hundred yards or more ahead with no lights showing. It turned in his direction and then the lights came on full beam, blinding him momentarily so that he slowed down still more.

The other car was barely moving as it passed him, and in his rear-view mirror he saw it pull over to the curb with its lights cut off again.

After that he dismissed it from his mind for the moment as he came abreast of the agency building easily identified by the sign outside. He parked his car in front of it, and went up the walk to the front door noting as he went the empty parking area in back of the building and wondering where Mrs. Blaine had left her car. She must have driven here, he thought. Her house was at least two miles away on the other side of town.

Lights shone from the building. He rang the bell and heard it echo emptily inside. He looked back up the street for the car that had passed him and then stopped.

Light car, he thought, as he rang the bell again. The Blaines had a pale blue Mercury. Was it theirs that had stopped right after it passed him? It had come out of a driveway somewhere around here. What had become of it, though? With no other cars moving along the street to distract his attention he would have noticed the lights going on if it had been driven away. It must still be parked where it had stopped. He strained his eyes for a glimpse of it among the trees that lined the sidewalk, a glint of its chrome from the nearest street light, but he could see no sign of it.

He rang the bell a third time long and hard and yet with a sense of futility. No one would answer it, he knew all at once, because there was no one inside. The lights that shone through the drawn blinds had been left turned on in an empty building—by Inez Blaine driving away from it in the car that had passed him a few minutes ago.

Madden's finger came off the bell with a jerk as if he'd received an electric shock from it. He'd had one of a different kind that came from the sudden realization of how wrong he had been in the picture he'd formed of the car that hit Lucia last fall. It was light, she'd said, and he'd pictured it as cream or gray or very light tan. But a pale blue car, running her down on a dark rainy night, would have been of no particular color, just light, as she had said. And tonight it had been the same thing. Seeing it from a distance coming out of a driveway, having it pass him in a glare of headlights, it had been a light car and that was all.

By the time he had completed this thought Madden was back in his car making a U-turn in the road, driving back at a snail's pace, searching the road ahead for the pale blue Mercury. When he came to what he thought was approximately the place where it had stopped at the curb he pulled over and shut off his motor.

A dark car, not the one he was looking for, came toward him. Its lights flashed on the stone gateposts across the street from Madden, on a tree directly opposite him, and then it was gone. He reached for the flashlight in the glove compartment, and hurried across the street. When he had passed the gateposts himself not many minutes ago the snow that had drifted against them had been smooth and clean. Now, the lights of the other car had revealed a tire mark clearly outlined in it.

When Inez came out of the driveway and saw a car approaching she turned on her lights. As soon as it passed

214

her she pulled over to the curb opposite the Bradford house, turned off her lights, and leaned over the seat to look at her passenger. Lucia hadn't stirred, she was still deep in unconsciousness or perhaps, Inez thought, already dead. Either way she was giving no trouble at the moment. Satisfied of this, Inez leaned out the window to see what had become of the car that had passed her. Nowhere in sight, it must have gone on around the corner, she thought.

She got out, ran over to the gateposts, and unhooked the chain that blocked the driveway. A moment later she was back in her car and, after a glance in both directions to make sure she had the street to herself, she drove across it into the driveway, stopping to hook the chain back in place and then following the long winding drive until she found herself under a porte-cochere that she could scarcely see in the darkness.

She could scarcely see anything at first when she got out of her car and began to move around in back of the house on a tour of exploration. The Bradfords were older people; she didn't know them well, had been in their house only two or three times in all the years her husband had worked in the bank, and couldn't remember ever having been outside on the grounds.

There were flower beds, specimen plantings, masses of shrubbery through which she picked her way, and at last, near the back door, found what she sought, a dense screen of evergreens behind which, with luck, Lucia's body might lie for days with nothing less than a thorough search revealing it.

She went back to the car and moved it forward to lessen the distance that she would have to drag the girl. Then she opened the back door and pulled her out, an inert burden.

Was she already dead?

If she wasn't, she would be in another few minutes. Then what?

Inez realized that she hadn't really thought that out yet. Strip her wallet, drop it beside her body to indicate a motive? Or would it be better to point toward a man by ripping her clothes as if she'd been the victim of an attempted sex attack?

Never mind about that now, she told herself. It could wait.

Cold madness had taken possession of her. Lucia no longer existed to her as a person, only as a disposal problem. She began to drag her across the frozen ground.

She was midway between the car and the clump of evergreens, lost to everything but the urgent task that engaged all her energies, when Madden, moving swiftly but silently, came around the corner of the house. He broke stride and stood stock still, chilled by what he saw, dreading its meaning, Inez with her burden, her labored breathing loud in the quiet.

"What are you doing, Mrs. Blaine?" he demanded.

She screamed as she looked up and caught sight of him, a tall silhouette against the sky. He looked twice his actual height to her, he had no identity, his voice was one she had never heard, the words he spoke carried no meaning, he was a faceless figure of menace, a black creature of legend from out of the night, he was retribution.

She screamed again at the top of her lungs, dropped her burden, and ran from him across the lawn, through shrubbery and flower beds, falling once, picking herself up and running on, incapable of thought, just running to get away from the figure that might have sprung up from out of the ground.

Madden didn't pursue her. He dropped down beside Lucia, not daring to hope that she still alive.

Inez, in her panic, plunged blindly into a clothes reel,

216

drew back to circle around it, ran on and on not knowing where she was, where she was going. She didn't see the perennial border with low wire wickets edging it, didn't know it was there until she tripped over a wicket and went headlong over the border, over the retaining wall down to the cement walk below. She screamed as she fell, screams of stark terror that would ring in Madden's ears long after the last of them ended in a shocking silence.

Chapter Twenty

Days passed before Lucia, in the hospital with a lineal skull fracture, was allowed to have any visitors. Her mother had come down from Lowell immediately on being notified of what had happened to her daughter and had all but lived at the hospital since.

Lucia lay in a state between coma and sleep most of the time at first, remembering little of what had brought her there, asking a minimum of questions, content to let each day take care of itself.

Rod was the first person she asked to see after she had become somewhat oriented to her surroundings. He was permitted a five-minute visit and didn't try to talk, just held her hand and smiled at her with a world of tenderness in his eyes. Thereafter, his visits increased in length, and by the end of the week Lucia, now much better, wanted him to tell her every detail of what had happened. But Rod had been instructed that she must have no excitement, that rest and quiet were what she needed most. He told her that Madden had saved her and that Inez Blaine was dead, killed in a fall while running away. The rest, he said, would have to wait until the inspector could tell it to her himself.

Lucia protested to her mother and doctor. "You can't

expect me to be quiet until I've heard the whole story. I want to see Inspector Madden."

The police hadn't been allowed to see her yet, but on her ninth day in the hospital her doctor said that Madden could. He went to the hospital with Rod and found her alert enough, her bandaged head supported by a single pillow, her eyes looking too big for her face.

She spoked disconsolately of her appearance. "They won't tell me how much of my hair they shaved off," she said. "I bet I'll have to go into hiding for weeks after I get out of here."

"Wear a cap," Rod suggested. "I could take that better than having you incommunicado."

She smiled at him. "I'll think it over."

The room was filled with flowers. Madden made the usual comments on how lovely they were, how much they added to a sickroom.

"Everyone's been sending them," she said. "I told Rod"—she gave him a fondly reproachful glance—"he'd be bankrupt if he didn't stop. Then they've been coming from people up home and just about everyone at the bank. Even Mr. Jenner," she concluded impishly.

"They won't bankrupt him," Madden observed.

"No." Her face clouded slightly as she looked at the inspector who was standing at the foot of her bed. "Now that we've gone through all the polite small talk won't you sit down, Inspector—and you, Rod—and tell me all about it?"

"All right." Madden pulled a chair around to face her, Rod sat down next to him.

"Rod's told you Mrs. Blaine is dead, that she broke her neck when she fell," Madden began.

"Yes." She paused. "He also told me that it's you I have to thank for saving my life."

There was warmth in the inspector's dark eyes as they rested on her. "I'll always be glad I was there when I was needed," he said gently, and then in a lighter tone, "Justifying my existence for once."

"From my point of view," Lucia said, keeping her tone as light as his had been at the end, "you've had a very full career."

"I'll go along with that!" Rod was fervent in agreement.

A little embarrassed, Madden eyed them smilingly. He told Lucia, "Your mother expressed the same sentiments when she came to see me the other day. That makes it unanimous, and no more time need be spent in discussion of it."

"Mother went to . . . ? She didn't tell me—oh, of course not." Lucia made a face. "No excitement for the patient." Her voice slowed as she went on, "It's hard to believe Mrs. Blaine hated me so much because of Gibb. I never dreamed—"

"Well, he was her whole life. Her husband didn't count."

"Poor Mr. Blaine," Lucia said softly. "He must feel terrible."

Madden's thoughts went to the talks he'd had with Alec Blaine, the dazed disbelief the other man displayed. "I don't think he's really taken it all in yet," he replied.

"I feel so sorry for him," Lucia said. "Such an empty life and now this. When I was going out with Gibb I used to wonder how Mr. Blaine put up with his wife. I didn't like her from the moment I met her. I saw how she bossed him around and would have done the same to Gibb, except that he wanted things his way just as much as she wanted them hers. And I couldn't help noticing how she was always on the make to better her social position by serving on committees and things. Oh dear—" Lucia gave a sigh. "I should shut up. She's dead now."

"She got exactly what was coming to her." Rod's glance went to Lucia's bandaged head.

"Yes, she did." Madden went on. "The best I can find to say of her is that she must have lived under a certain amount of strain trying to keep up with Fairmount's elite. From what her husband told me, she came from a very poor home herself and never stopped worrying about getting a foothold on the next rung up the ladder."

Lucia nodded. "You could sense that in her right away. Although she was very nice to me when I first went out with Gibb."

"Sure she was," Madden said. "Your father was the president of a bank."

"Yes, that was it." The girl divided a sober glance between them. "Lying here with nothing else to do, I've been thinking about the car that hit me. It was only about three weeks after Gibb left."

"We'll never know and there's no point in thinking about it," Madden said firmly.

Rod agreed with him and added, "You've got enough to think about without that."

Lucia summoned a smile. "I'm outnumbered."

A moment later she wanted to bring up the night Inez tried to kill her, but they told her no, she mustn't talk about that yet.

"All right, I know," she said. "I'm not to get excited. I don't think I would, anyway. It's still not quite real to me, beginning with the moment I saw the typewriter." She looked at Madden. "Will you please tell me, though, why she thought she could get away with using it?"

He told her what he had learned from Mrs. Burdett about the new typewriter at the agency. The portable, rarely used since the new machine was purchased, had been taken out of the closet that Monday afternoon by Mrs. Burdett because the other typewriter happened to be in use. Then she had neglected her intention to put it away before she went home. "So you see," he said, "the portable wasn't such a risk after all."

222

"But if I hadn't seen it, you'd have caught her some other way," Lucia observed. "Rod says postal inspectors keep working on cases until they're cleared up."

A twinkle came into Madden's eyes as he glanced at Rod. "Haven't you told her about our failures?"

"Of course not," Rod replied. "I'm building up the POD to her, not tearing it down."

"How else could you have caught her?" Lucia persisted.

The inspector hesitated, wondering how much of the story he ought to tell her at present. Enough, he thought, to remove any impression that the Service needed such deplorable short cuts as attempted murder to achieve results.

He gave her a brief account of the steps he had taken to catch Inez Blaine mailing one of the letters, his reluctance to make a move toward the typewriter for fear of frightening her off, only to find, through her failure to mail one that last Monday, that she seemed to have been already frightened off—at least temporarily.

Then he told her about the references made to an incident long ago in Newton, Pennsylvania, involving someone at the bank, and outlined his efforts to track down the source of the information.

Discovering that hospital chairs were not designed for lounging, he stood up and wandered around the room as he talked.

"Mrs. Blaine was dead by the time that point was cleared up. Mrs. Chapin didn't want to say much at first, but when she found out from the Pittsburgh inspector how serious the case was she admitted that she got acquainted with Mrs. Blaine at Bar Harbor last summer and told her the story. It seems that at the time it happened she was going out with the man involved in it. So you see . . ." Madden propped himself against the wall, hands in his pockets, his gaze fixed on Lucia.

A moment later, he continued, "I found other mistakes of Mrs. Blaine's at the VNA. She'd not only used a typewriter that it wouldn't do her any good to get rid of because I could get samples from it all over the place, but she also used their paper; and in a drawer she reserved for personal things I found a supply of the envelopes she mailed the letters in."

He came to a halt. Lucia said, "I don't think I'll take up poison pen letters. There's so much that can give you away. And other post offices helping to catch you too."

"All over the country as needed," Madden said.

"One great big happy team?"

He grinned. "Well, not quite that ideal. We have our differences too."

"Just the same, I'll still keep away from poison pen," Lucia declared.

"Be awkward for Rod if you didn't," he suggested teasingly.

"Turn her in myself," Rod said, giving her a fond look.

The look she returned to him was equally fond. But a little tired, Madden thought. They were staying too long.

He went over to the bed, took her hand in both of his, and said with a smile, "Other questions can wait. Hurry up and get better."

"Hurry up and get my hair to grow too," she said.

"Never mind," Rod said. "Without a hair on your head you'd still look good to me."

Madden, laughing, left them to have a few minutes alone together and went out into the corridor to wait for Rod.